THE GANGST

CHAPTER ONE.

PART ONE.

THE LOST LEADER.

A volley of shots rang out in a street in Paris. Four men came running along the pavement, pausing occasionally to shoot into the darkness. They piled into a waiting car.

At the very last moment, as the car sped forward, a fifth man came staggering out of an alleyway, made a terrific effort and jumped on to the running board.

Willing hands clutched him and hauled him inside. He sank back with a gasp as the car rapidly reached seventy miles an hour. Through Paris they roared like a runaway comet, but the man who had arrived last was playing very little heed to his whereabouts.

There was a big bloodstain rapidly spreading over his chest. He kept one had to the wound, and smiled rather grimly when one of the four tried to prop him in a more comfortable position.

"No use Slim. They've got me this time. Too near the heart for comfort. I won't last another half-hour."

The car ran over the edge of the pavement as it turned down a side street. The man at the wheel was a brilliant driver. Those inside did not even look up. Their eyes were fixed on the face of the big, bronzed man who was dying in their midst.

"Boss, you can't mean it! Lets drive to a doctor," suggested a tall, slender man, whose dandified appearance was in marked contrast with the sweaters and mufflers of the others.

"No Slim," the dying man ordered, "Drive on into the country. Just because the police got me there's no reason why you should be copped. If you go back into Paris you'll be nabbed, and in any case, no doctor can do anything for me. I've had a good run for my money. Tonight's raid would have been the biggest haul of our careers if it had come off."

"Scarface!"

It was a short, swarthy man who now spoke, leaning over the dying man with one hand braced against the door to prevent himselffrom swaying with the car.

"What's going to happen with the gang when your gone? Who's going to be our chief?"

Scarface Shale smiled bitterly.

"Don't ask me to chose. Settle that amongst youselves. Slim or you Nick, are the two best men I have. One of you ought to take command. Don't let the grizzlies down."

The car had come to a halt in a dark lane. The driver evidently considered that he had safely shaken off the police who had attempted to follow them from the Rue de la Paix, where the raid on a famous jeweller's shop had taken place. He came to the door to help lift out the shot leader.

They placed him gently on a motor rug and he gazed up at the twinkling stars with a yearning look in his hard eyes.

"Listen boys," he muttered, so softly that they had to stoop to hear him, "We've got on well together, eh? I've neer let you down, and you've never let me down. We've all lined our pockets pretty well since the gang was started."

There was a grunt of agreement from the gansters. Vicious crooks though they were, their faces softened as they looked down on Scarface Shale.

The moon peeped out from behind the clouds, and for a moment showed the livid scar across Shale's forehead. It had been a clancing wound made by a scrap of shrapnel during the war. It had given him his nickname when out of sheer craving for excitement he had become the leader of this gang of criminals.

"And you won't let me down after I'm dead?" he queried, rising on one elbow.

"What do you mean, chief?" It was Slim Dolman who spoke, "How can we?"

"Well I've never told you lads that I've a son. His mane's Tom, and he's at St Ardens School, one of the most famous boys schools in England. He doesn't know a thing about me, or how I get my money. His mother died when he was young, and I've been everything to him. He has no suspicion that his father is the head of the most succesful gang in Europe. Understand?"

They nodded. Someone gave him a drink, and he gulped it greedily. He seemed to know he was racing against time.

"Well, if you lads promise never to let Tom know about me, there is only one more thing you can do for me. In th Lyons Bank I've enough money to see the boy through the rest of his education, and to set him up in life. Swear to me that you'll see he gets the money. Swear!"

Their hands shot forward and met. Fingers interlaced, palms crossed, they repeated the gang oath, and the dying man sank back as though satisfied.

"There's a note for him sewn in the lining of my jacket. I've carried it for a long time. Don't let him have it unless things go wrong. Just let him think his father died as a result of a car accident in Paris. Make the rest of the gang understand this, will you?"

Again they nodded, and Captain Shale, better known as Scarface Shale, closed his eyes for the last time.

Three minutes later the gangsters had finished emptying his pockets and securing the note he had mentioned. Nick Stiebel thrust this into his wallet.

"Well he was the best leader a gang ever had, and I'm sorry to see him go. There's nothing we can do for him. No use thinking of taking the body. The cops will bury him when they find him."

Slowly, their hats in their hands, the gangsters filed back into the car, and drove rapidly away by a roundabout road which brought them back to Paris on the opposite side.

In the back room of a cheap cafe they met the rest of their comrades, and broke the bad news to them. Not only had the night's raid failed, but their trusted leader was dead.

It was obvious from the low-voiced comments that Scarface had been a leader in a million. Everyone regretted his going, but nevertheless there was the matter of their choosing a new gang leader to be faced.

Nick Stiebel's thin lips curled back from his yellow teeth.

"Well, who's it going to be? Scarface said either Slim or me. What about putting it to the vote?"

After some argument they agreed on this, and when the votes were counted it was found they had six votes each. The gang was equally split, half for Slim Dolman and the other half for Nick Stiebel. Already the death of Scarface the Grizzlies with division.

They argued for an hour or more faces grew flushed, hands moved towards pockets where guns and knives were kept and the situation was an ugly one. It was Nick

Stiebel who again took the floor.

"Boys, it's not worth it. We're going to wreck the whole gang this way. The Grizzlies will go to pieces if we quarrel. Niether Slim or me can be chief, but luckily there's a third choice none of us can grumble at."

"Who's that, Nick?" demanded the crowd eagerly.

Nick Stiebel produced from his pocket the envelope which was addressed—"Tom Shale, Sixth Form, St Ardens School, Brightliinton, England." Three times he jerked his forefinger at the address, and his meaning slowly sank in.

"The kid! Scarface's son!" Slim Dolman replied, "Come off that Nick! Scarface made me promise we would never get the kid mixed up with the gang."

"Bah!" Nick snarled his contempt, "I promised along with the rest of you, didn't I? And I mean to keep my promise. But Scarface never guessed we were going to be in danger of a split, or he would have suggested the kid himself."

"I don't believe it!" Slim Dolman towered over his shorter rival, "Scarface never intended that kid to know a thing about his dad's job in life. I'm for keeping him out of it. He's at one of the finest schools in England, and it's not fair to bring him in with us."

Several of the gangsters growled approval of Slim's views, but it was clear that Nick Siebel was by no means convinced.

"Sentiment! That's all it is. We'll be doing the kid a good turn by making him the chief of the Grizzlies in succession to the father. Besids—" he smacked his lips, "Don't forget he's at a high class school, where all the swells send their kids."

"What about it?" growled Slim, his usually pale face red and flushed.

"Don't you see our chance? The sons of millionaires and all kinds of nobs go to that school. It's a soft thing for us to work the kidnapping racket there once we've got Tom Shale in our gang. It'll be money for jam. It'll be dead easy."

Slim and two of the others started to protest, but they were shouted down. Nick had scored a master stroke when he mentioned about the opportunity for kidnapping, tired and a desire for easy money was the one thing which kept the gang together, and they were almost dazzled of the prospect thrown before them.

There and then they decided that young Tom Shale of the Saint Ardens School, England should be persuaded or forced to take over the leadership of the Grizzles in succession to his father.

By three different cross-Channel routes the gang crossed to England the next morning.

PART TWO.

THE MYSTERY MESSAGES.

"There's the blighter again. Look!"

As he spoke Dick Seymour stooped grabbed a stone, and hurled it with all his might at the head which was just ducking down behind the quadrangle wall. The stone struck a splinter of moss-grown wall, but the face disappeared just in time.

"Good shot," chuckled Tom Shale, "Your coming on with your over-arm work, young Seymour. But what's the spite against the fellow?"

"He's been hanging around here for a couple of days now. Twice I've seen him peering over the wall. Maybe we aught to tell the Don about him."

Tom Shale brought down his big hand with a thud between his pal's shoulder-blades. The captain of St Ardens was by far the biggest and strongest boy in the school, and a slapon the back from him was not to be lightly regarded.

Dick spluttered, coughed, and aimed a swinging blow at his companion's smiling face.

"Cheese it! Trying to wind me? S I was saying—."

"Aw, forget it, Dick. Don't get the windup because some old tramp looks over the wall. Coming down to the footer field? I want to look over these old boots of mine they're getting hard."

"Can't be done. I've got to do some chemistry exercises. I want to get that off my chest. See you when you come back."

"Righto, don't get your nose in the ink!"

Tom Shale was humming to himself as he turned under the elms towards the gateway. It still wanted two hours to last bell, and the evening was fairly warm for the time of the year.

With his hands in his pockets, and his cap perched on the back of his head, big Tom Shale looked the picture of fitness and contentment. The school was proud of him. Very few could say they had as few enemies as he had.

As he neared the gate his thoughts were full of the forthcoming football match with Hazelton College.

Thud!

Someone had thrown a stone over the wall, and it had only missed him by a yard. There it lay on the paving, and even from where he stood he could see that a piece of paper was wrapped round it. He stooped to pick it up.

"What silly ass is trying to be funny?" he wondered as he smoothed out the paper, "Hello, it's addressed to me!"

It was printed in pencilled letters in sprawling fashion across the whole paper.

"To Tom Shale. If you want to hear of something which concerns you very much come to the cattle shed at the corner of Farmer Blatchard's field after six. Do not fail."

Tom turned it this way and that, held it up to the light and finally screwed it up into a ball. There was a grin on his face when he passed through the gateway.

As he expected, there was nobody in sight, but there were plenty of trees nearby, where the unknown thrower of the stone could have bolted to.

"Someone's trying to pull my leg," he muttered, "Must be one of the Lower Form, kids, to think I'd be soft enough to go to Blatchard's field. I'll swish him if I ever find out who chucked it."

Japes of this kind, attempted and otherwise were not unknown to Tom. He had taken part in his share of them, and had suffered his share of the consequences. But hehad no intention of making a mug of himself by visiting the cattle shed.

He promptly dismissed thethe matter from his mind, and made his way across the football field to the pavilion. There had been heavy rain recently, and the ground was too soft to play. Being a prefect, he had a key to the pavilion, but was rather surprised to find the door already unlocked.

"Some careless blighter forgot to lock it after him," he mumbled, "Some tramp might come in and pinch all he wanted."

All the senior boys had their own lockers, and their names on cards and slipped into slots on the doors of these lockers. Tom Shale's hand was already out to open his when he paused. Pinned to the front of his locker was a paper, and even in the poor light of the pavilion he could read—.

"To Tom Shale:- You are urgently required to visit the old cattle shed at the corner of Farmer Blatchard's field after six o'clock. Consequences will be serious if you do not turn up. The matter concerns your father."

Tom's mouth tightened.

A jape was all very well, but why bring his father into it?

"Blithering idiots! I've a good mind to lead Dick and a few of the others over here to give them the shock of their lives. That grubby handwriting looks like something the Lower Fourth would do."

He ripped off the paper, opened his locker, and attended to the boots, as he had intended. A good greasing would soften them a lot.

Altogether he was there for more than half an hour, locked up, walked briskly back to the school, and went at once to his study. There was still an hour before roll-call, and he had been halfway through a rather exciting detective novel. It lay on the table near his favourite armchair, and a few moments later he was sprawling at ease, ready for a quiet hour's read.

The book opened readily in the middle, but instead of his usual bookmark a sealed envelope fell out. It was addressed to him by name, and when he opened it, the captain of St Ardens sat bolt upright with a snort of disgust.

"This is getting a bit thick! The cheek of the rotters!"

It was another of those crudely-printed notes repeating the invitation to the cattle shed, and adding that unless he turned up he would never learn the truth about his father.

If there had not been this impertinent mention of his father he would have thrown it on the fire, but Tom that this was getting past a joke. He and his father were the best of pals, and he thought that there was no finer man in all the world. He could not stand having his name banded about by a joker.

"I'll go, and I'll make 'em sorry I ever came," he grunted, and armed himself with a prefect's cane, slipping it up his sleeve so that it would not be noticeable as he crossed the quad.

It was dusk, and most of the boys were wending their way back to the school. Dick Seymour would still be hard at work over his chemistry exercises, or Tom might have invited him to join the expedition. Not that he minded being alone. He felt quite capable of dealing with the jokers, no matter if there were three or four of them.

Wisely he took a roundabout way, keeping behind the hedges, and coming in upon the far end of the Blatchard's field from the further side. The cattle shed had been abandoned for some years, and the door was generally padlocked. Now he could see that the lock was off. That indicated he had not come on a wild goose chase. There was someone in there.

As he approached the door he sniffed. He could smell cigerette smoke. He frowned at that. It was like Lower Fourth boys to sneak out here and smoke.

With a sudden rush, he kicked the door open and jumped inside, cane in hand, ready for action.

Then his arm fell to his side, he gasped in bewilderment. Grouped about the shed were eight or nine tough-lookingmen and one had immediately between him and the door. He was a short, swarthy man, with a tight rat-trap mouth and a limp. His eyes were fixed unpleasantly on the youngster.

"Tom Shale is that your name?"

"Yes, but—."

"Gad you answered our notes. Sit down."

He motioned to an upturned box, whilst the rest of the men crowded round, cigarettes in mouth, as they stared at the youngster.

"It saves us a lot of bother, I'll come to business at once. It's about your father. He's dead."

"Dead!" gasped Tom, very glad he had sat down, "It can't be true. He's in Paris. I had a letter from him on Monday, and—."

"He was shot by the police on Tuesday evening whilst trying to burgle a jewellery store in the Rue de la Paix," said the man with the limp, "We were there when he died and he gave us this for you."

"Police—shot—dead!"

it was well Tom was sitting down, for the note he now readwas enough to knock anyone off his balance. It was a confession from his father, telling how a craving for excitement and a fancied grudge against society had led him into the realms of crime. It told how for years he had led this well-organised gang of crooksin robberies and other crimes all over Europe.

The letter ended this way.

"I can assure you, Tom, that we never commited murder, and only killedin self defence. We never robbed the poor. That's a wretched excuse, I know, but I have done my best for you, and you will have an education and money to give you a good start in the world. Think of me sometimes, and try to forgive—your father."

Tom's eyes were moist by the time he had finished, but he did not blink. Not for nothing was he captain of St Ardens.

"I see," he tried to control his voice, "It's my father's handwriting sure enough, but why have I been brought here? If you were his friends, why didn't you post the letter to me?"

This time it was the tall, slim dandy who leaned towards him.

"We wanted to tell you, kid, that you've inherited us. You've got to be our leader in your father's place. It's like this. I'm Slim Dolman, and I thought I was next in the running. That little runt on your other side is Nick Stiebel, and he thinks he's entitled to be the next leader. If we argue it out we'll bust up the gang, and that'll be a shame. We're making too good a thing out of it. So the boys decided that the son of Scarface Shale would be our leader. The name of Shale is big name in the world where we move, and it would be a big advantage to us to have the son of our old chief as our leader. Here's to you chief."

He held out his hand towards the astonished Tom, and every man in the shed did the same. Flushed faces, pale faces, evil faces, and some not so bad looking, were all turned towards the trembling boy.

Tom swayed on his feet. His head was in a whirl.

"I won't do it. It's impossible. You can take your gang and drown it for all I care. I won't be made a crook."

Half-a-dozen men reached for their guns as though to use them, but Nick Stiebel was already on his feet.

"Chief, you don't understand. If you turn us down we shall consider you a traitor, and there's only one rule for traitors in our crowd—death! There's something else. Your father kept his secret from everyone, and all his friends think he was an honest fine man. Well he was a good sort, and it would hurt us to have the fact that he was a master crook. I guess you'll take on the job alright."

Tom gared round with clenched fists. These men were deadly serious. They were willing to follow and obey him, but they were not willing to let him go out of their lives. He had been chosen as their leader, and to refuse meant death for himself and disgrace for his name.

He was as brave as any lad of eighteen, and as big as most of the men there, but he certainly felt himself trembling.

Then he drew a deep breath. Why should he not pretend to fall in with their wishes and accept their leadership, but if he led them it would be for his own ends and not for theirs.

"Alright, I'll do it, but I can't stop here any longer. I've got to get back to the school in time for the last bell. Otherwise I'll be missed and questions will be asked."

"Righto chief," grinned Stiebel, "Go back to your school, and we'll keep in touch with you. You follow your father's footsteps, that's all we ask. When we want your help we'll get it, and maybe it won't be long before a job crops up. Got a gun?"

He pushed an automatic towards Tom, but the lad shoved it back.

"What use have I got for a thing like that? He demanded.

Like one in a dream, he found himself walking back by the familiar path. His father's letter was still in his pocket. He must burn it when he got to his room. He had become a gangster chief without wishing to be one. One day he would be leading the school eleven and the next day a pack of crooks. It was fantastic.

How he got through the rest of the evening he never knew. It was with relief that he finally got to bed and shut himself upwith his thoughts. Even when sleep came it was troubled, and about two hours after he had closed his eyes he found himself wide awake again. Someone stood by his bedside.

Tom Shale had found someone in his room at dead of noght before that. Midnight japes were not unknown at St Ardens, and his first conclusion was that a prank was being played on him, so, instead of jumping up in alarm, he softly reached for the glass of water which stood on the chair beside him. That in the face of the would be japer should dampen the success of the little plot.

Slight as the rustle of his pjamas was, it was heard by the dim figure at his side.

"Chief," said a voice, "Don't make a sound. It's me—Max. I'm one of the gang, and I've got a message for you."

PART THREE

THE FIRST CRIME.

Tom Shale went and cold by turns. For the moment he had quite forgotten about the gang. Only two hours ago he had been thinking over the awful situation in which he found himself, but sleep had taken the memory from his mind. Now it all came back with a rush.

He sat up.

"What do you want? How did you get in here? You shouldn't have done it. If anyone hears—."

"They won't hear. Think I don't know my job, chief?" came the aggrieved voice of the gangster, "You sleep with your windows open, and I'm the best cat-burgler in England. So why wonder how I got in? Sorry to disturb you, but it's importnt. It cropped up after you left, and it concerns this school."

Tom tiptoed to the door and locked it. He felt better after that.

"How can anything about the school concern you?"

"Easy! There's a kid here name of Standers, Hiram Standers junior."

"Yes, an American boy in the Fourth, but—."

"That's the one. After you left we heard from one of our agents that Hiram Standers senior had just reached Southampton, and in an interview with one of the reporters, he confessed that he was one of the richest men in the states, and that he was over here to visit his son."

"Well I could have told you all that. The kid is always bragging about his father's money."

Max smacked his lips loudly

"And we never knew it. Well, this is what's going to happen. Before the father gets here the kid is going to get kidnapped and held to ransom. His father will pay anything to get him released. All you've got to do is to tell us exactly wher he sleeps."

Tom Shale went cold with horror. So this was the sort of thing he was going to be mixed up in, kidnapping! Ransom! He knew the Amercan boy well. He was a youg cad, who, in Tom's opinion, desarved a dozen with the cricket stump every morning until he lost his own sense of importance, but that did not mean to say he should be kidnapped and held to ransom.

"I'll be darned if I will!" he snorted, raising his voice louder than he intended.

Max opened his mouth, then closed it again. Outside in the corridor there was a footstep. As quick as sight the gangster glided to the door, unlocked it, then with a quick sign to the startled Tom dived under the bed.

He was not a moment too soon. Tom was barely under the bedclothes when the door softly opened,Price, the mathematics master quietly entered.

Tom gave a grunt and sat up rubbing his eyes.

"Who's that?" he asked sharply.

Mr Price turned on the light and blinked at him through his horn-rimmed spectacles.

"What was that talking I herd in here Shale?"

"Talking! Talking in here, sir, but—."

"I thought I heard voices. Have you had any of the other boys in here?" the master was staring about him intently, and every moment Tom was thinking he might look under the bed.

"You know it is strictly against the rules, and that you as captain should—."

"But, I have no boys in here ,sir," protested Tom indignatly, "Maybe I was snoring a little."

"Huh, maybe I was mistaken, but it would be a very serious matter if a boy of your standing was found to have broken the school rules," growled the mathematics master, and left the room.

Not till his footsteps had vanished down the corridor did Tom mop his face.

"Phew, that was a close one! He creeps round at nights and listens for trouble."

Max came crawling out from under the bed, there was a gun in his hand.

"The old skunk! Tell you what I'll do, chief, I'll slip along after him and bump him off."

He was almost at the door, when Tom hauled him back. The idea of "bumping off" the maths master in such a cool fashion quite knocked him off his balance. Max was quite reluctant to come back into the room and give up the idea.

"Well?" demanded the gangster, "Where does this kid sleep? We're going to get him tonight. Four of the boys are outside with a car. Which room and which bed."

Tom Shale did some quick thinking. He was certainly not going to let them have Hiram Standers. He was not going to be mixed up in any kidnapping.

He remembered there was an empty room near the Fourth Form dormitory. It was detached from the others, and was sometimes occupied by one of the junior masters. Just now it was vacant.

"Well, because of his money he's got a room to himself," he told the unsuspecting Max, who eveidently knew very little about English public school life. "It's at the end of the next corridor. The last door on the right. But if you make a noise you'll have the whole dormitory awake."

"Huh, we'll wake nobody!" grunted Max, making for the door, "I'll just slip down and let the boys in. we won't be to minutes over the job. A whiff of chloroform and a bag over his head will do the trick. We'll be out again in five minutes."

He was gone again as silently as a shadow, but he could not have been at the head of the staircase before Tom was into his dressing-gown and stealing out along the corridor. He had made up his mind what to do.

The room he had mentioned wasin darkness and the door was unlocked. He did not go inside, but merely put his hand round the edge, removed the key from the inside and put it in the lock in readiness on the outside.

Then he drew back into the alcove leading to the Fourth Form dormitory.

Not four minutes elapsed before three stealthy figures came up the stairs and down the corridor. They had felt pads on their feet and made no sound at all.

One shone a light on the door of the empty room and nodded. A moment later they were gliding through the open doorway and closing it behind them.

That was Tom's chance. As quick as lightening he reached out and turned thekey, locking them in. then he whirled about and rushed into the Fourth Form dormitory.

"Hi, you chaps, quickly! Grab cricket stumps or something. I've just seen three burglars go into Number Eighteen. I've locked them in."

His excited voice shattered the sleep of the twenty boys who occupied the dormitory. Inside half a minute they were all scrambling out of bed, grabbing the first suitable weapon they could find. All stampeding towards the door in their eagernass to get a swipe at the burglars.

Tom kept back. He intended Max and theothers to get caught, but he did not intend to be seen by them in the forefront. He wanted the rest of the gang to believe it was an accident.

He saw the boys charge the locked door before they thought of turning the key. From inside came strange sounds, and the creaking of a bed. Someone close to Tom Shale muttered—.

"Old Price won't half get a shock."

"What's that?" the school captain grabbed his arm, "What's that young Brown? Is Mr Price in there? It's not his room. It was empty and—."

"Old Price moved in there this evening, I saw him. Said he could keep a closer watcg on us if he moved to number eighteen. I hope he's having heart failure. Whoops!"

The door had been flung wide open at last, the electric light switched on, and a dozen younsters poured into the room, waving their assorted weapons. Down the corridor came running the porter and Holford, the science master. The noise had disturbed them.

But nobody heeded their coming. Tom Shale and the rest of the boys were staring at an open window. It was a good thirty feet to the ground, but a rope hung down, the upper end attached to the bed. The gangsters had made their escape that way, and as Tom reached the window he heard a car start up in the road beyond.

Max and the other had made a quick getaway, and they had not gone empty handed. The bed was disordered as though by a struggle. Mr Price was no longer there.

"They've got old Price! He's been kidnapped!" arose the shout, "Mr Price has been kidnapped and carried away in a car."

Tom Shale turned his head to hide the startled expression on his face. How was he to know Mr Price had moved his room? How was he to know would operate in the dark, and mistake the maths master for the American boy they had come for.

It had all been a hideous mistake. How was it going to end? What would the Grizzlies do when they discovered what had happened.

The son of Scarface clenched his hands tightly in his dressing-gown pocket. What a mess

CHAPTER TWO.

PART ONE.

SCHOOL CAPTAIN AND GANG LEADER.

"Shale, see that none of the boys leave their dormitories again tonight. I give you the responsibility of keeping them out of the way of the poice."

Dr Limley, the headmaster of St Ardens, looked worried and flustered. There was a very good reason for it. Never in the history of the school had anything like this happened before. Mr Price, the mathematics master, had been kidnapped in the middle of the night by three unknown men, who had entered the school and carried hime away in a car.

The police had been quickly phoned. Already two detectives and three constables were in the building.

The excitement amonst the boys was intense. They had all hated Mr Price, who was a sneak and a general mischief-maker. They were thrilled rather than sorry at what had happened, and it was certainly going to be a handful even for big Tom Shale, the captain of the school, to keep them in order.

But Tom was glad of the opportunity to have something to do. He quickly sorted them out and with other prefects chased them back to their dormitories. It would do the police no good to have several hundred boys running round the place.

"I'll lick anyone who shows his head outside the door again," he growled as he shut the door of the Fourth Form dormitory.

They knew he meant it. Tom Shale was as fair a captain of a school as could be, but he never broke his word. If he promised a fellow a licking that fellow would get it, good and hard. The Fourth Form discussed the situation in very suddued whispers after Tom had gone.

If they could have seen Tom Shale's face once he was alone in the corridor they might have wondered.

"Phew! Of all the messes!" he muttered.

For out of all the people in St Ardens the captain was the only one who knew just what had happened. The kidnapping of the master was his fault.

It was all a ghastly business, and it had began with a terrible discovery that his father had been shot by the poice in Paris whilst leading a gang of crooks called the Grizzlies. Tom had always believed his father to be an honest man, and it was only after his death that he had discovered that Scarface Shale was the leader of this notorious European gang.

The gang had got in touch with him, and had ordered him to act as their leader, for oherwise there were one or two claiments for the job who would cause the whole gang to quarrel and break up.

Tom Shale had found himself in the ridiclous position of inheriting a gang. He had protested and argued, but they had threatened not only to expose his dead father, but to shoot him if he did not eccept the job. Finally Tom had been forced in to it, but he had taken the leadership with the intention in his mind to put his wit against theirs.

That night they had asked him to help them to kidnap the son of a millionaire who was in the school. He had told them the wrong room, believing it empty, and by mistake they had kidnapped Mr Price.

It was no wonder that the captain of the school was worried.

He paced the corridors, hearing the swish of a cane and the sharp cries of the younsters in the third form dormitory. That would be his pal Dick Seymour, trying to persuade some of the rebellious kids to go to bed and not hang out of the windows.

He wished he could tell Dick. But how could a fellow be the respected captain of his school and at the same time the head of a gang of criminals?

He carefully avoided the corridor where the masters and the police were talking. He did not want to face anyone in his present mood. He was only wondering what the gang would say when they found out their mistake.

He stopped by one of the windows at the end nearest the empty common-room in order to stare out at the night. It was the back of the quad, and he could not see the police cars which were parked at the front. The night was very dark.

He could imagine the kidnapper's car speeding through the lanes towards the headquarters of the Grizzlies. It was rather funny to think of old Price muffled in a blanket, and doubtless believing it was a schoolboy jape from which he was suffering.

Tap-tap! The knock on the window came almost from under Tom's nose. He jumped back faintly seeing a moving figure. He could only see it dimly, but the person out there could see him clearly, for he was in the light.

An electric torch came on, not upon Tom, bit upon the face of the man outside.

Tom recognised it at once. The swarthy, thin-lipped face was that of Nick Stiebel, one of the chief members of the gang. He had so far shown no friendly spirit towards the younster.

Tom cautiously lifted the lower part of the window. He was shaking with excitement, rather than fear. The cool night air gushed in, the light had gone out.

"Ssssssh!" came the sharp hiss, "Come out here, if you know what's good for you."

Tom scowled. If he was caught climbing out of a window when he had been left in charge of the junior boys there would be trouble. But he dare not disappoint the gangster now.

Deftly he swung one leg over the sill and dropped outside. In the darkness, after the light, he was quite blind. A hand closed on his elbow and led him in amonst the laurels that formed a wide patch in front of Dr Lumley's own quarters.

"What was the meaning of playing that joke on us?" hissed Stiebel bitterly, "We found out soon after leaving here. Hs language wasn't that of a kid. What's the idea? He says he's a master here."

"So he is. It was a mistake. He took that room tonight, and I knew nothing about it. What have you done with him?"

The hand released it's hold. He could see another man on the other side of him. The gang had been swift to follow uptheir discovery.

"Him! Oh! We chucked him out in a ditch beyond the village somewhere. I would have shot him if I'd had my way. Slim Dolman was too chicken-hearted. He always is. That's not the point. We've got to get hold of that American kid quickly. He's still in the school, and you'll know where he is."

Tom's heart thumped madly. Of course he knew where Hiram Standers, the young American whose father was so immensly wealthy slept. The gang wanted him for ransom, but Tom was just as determined they should not get him.

"The school is in an uproar," he muttered, "The poice are there, detectives, and all kinds of people. It'll be too dangerous."

"Aw, dead easy!" growled Nick Stiebel, and there was an ominous click as he cocked his revolver, "They're too busy looking for clues to see us. Shall we come in this way?"

He moved towards the window, and Tom jerked him back.

"Don't be a fool! If I don't get back and close that window someone will feel a draught and come to see. Ssh!"

He had just heard voices inside the corridor. Dr Lumley was raised louder than the rest.

"Look! A window open. Hat must be how the scoundrels got in in the first place, it's always fastened at night. I see to it myself. Maybe you can find footprints outside."

a uniformed figure came to the window and peered out, but was displaced by a plain-clothes detective, who shone his torchdownwards on to the soft flower-beds below. Nick Stiebel and the other gangster pulled Tom deeperinto the shrubbery. The next moment the dective spoke.

"Yes I see footptints, but only one set. Someone got out here recently."

He slid over the sill and stooped to examine the footprints more closely.

"That's queer!" he muttered, "Looks like slippers. No sane kidnapper would come here in slippers. Sure one of the boys hasn't got out to nose around. Doctor?"

Dr Lumley scowled. Tom heard his teeth set with that ominous click which always showed that he was in a fierce temper.

"Impossible! If it was one of the boys I would give him the flogging of his life. The prefects are all seeing that the boys keep to their dormitories. Can't you follow the fotprints, man?"

The dective looked hurt.

"Easy enough on the flower-bed, but here they get on to the turf and that's too dry and solid to take any marks. Maybe he's hidding in the shrubs. I can't see any sign of him having come back."

He shone the beam of light around the shrubbery, but without effect. Dr Lumley leaned out and called:-.

"If there's a boy out there let him show himself at once. I give him this last chance before I lock the window. Do you hear me?"

Tom could not help trembling. He could not have moved even if he had wanted, for someone had him by the arm, and he could feel something hard pushed against his ribs.

The silence aggravated the Doctor still more. He called the detective in, closed the window, and fastened both catches. Then he pulled down the blind.

"That's that," muttered the gangster with Stiebel.

Tom Shale dragged himself loose.

"Now look at the mess you've got me into, I'm locked out. The captain of the school locked out. How am I going to explain that? The Doctor will—."

"Aw, forget it," growled Stiebel, "We can open any door you want opened. I can see it's no use talking about kidnapping the American kid tonight. There are too many bulls and cops about. We'll have to leave it till another time. Now, which way do you want to get in?"

Tom pointed to a nearby side door. He knew it was locked on the inside, but Nick Stiebel took something from his pocket, fiddled at the lock for no more than two minutes and then opened the door wide.

"Here you are ,chief. Close it after you, and nothing will be known. Better clean those slippers before you go in, or they might spot the mud. So long. I'll tell the gang it wasn't your fault about the affair tonight, but expect to hear from us again soon. We've got to pull off a decent job to keep the home fires burning."

He vanished with his companion into the darkness, and Tom took his advice and cleaned his slippers thoroughly on the mat. On tiptoe he gained the other corridor, climbed the back stairs, and was near the Fourth Form dormitoty door when Dr Lumley almost bumped into him.

"Ah, here you are Shale. I was going to ask if any boy missing from here?"

"No sir. I feel sure they are all there.," gasped Tom, "Why sir?"

"I had a suspicion that a boy was outside the school. I found one of the lower windows open. Maybe I was wrong. Goodnight Shale. I think everything will be quiet now."

The captain of St Ardens tottered to his room. He felt he needed a sleep after all this.

PART TWO.

RECIEVER OF STOLEN GOODS.

The affair was a three day wonder. The next morning an early travelling postman heard the groans of Mr Price in the ditch and rescued him. Except for a bad cold the master was none the worse for his experience, although he told lurid stories of a desperate fight with ten gangsters who threatened to kill him.

One thing he did mention was that one of the kidnappers had let him realise that he was kidnapped in error. It was young Hiram Standers they had wanted. This had the effect of causing Standers' father to at once remove him from the school, and Tom Shale breathed more easily. At keast the Grizzlies could not make him go on with that business.

During the next few days some of the schoolboys must have thought their captain was ill. He was absent-minded, curt, and did not seem to have much interest in anything. Dick Seymour and Reddy Trotter, his special pals, noticed and remarked on it.

"Anyone would think you'd committed a murder and were waiting for them to find the body," said Reddy cheerfully.

Tom forced a grin.

"Can't a fellow feel down in the dumpssometimes? There's nothing the matter with me. Let's go up to the village. I want to buy a new pair of footie boots."

They made their shopping expedition, dropped in at their favourite tearoom for tea and cakes, for it was a half-holiday, and found a good many of their fellow schoolboys. There was a good deal of traffic passing, and it was quite interesting to watch it.

Suddenly a car swung out from a side road at high speed, swerved to avoid collision with an oncoming lorry, grazed it, and shot over the pavement. Crash! It hit the lamp-post outside the teashop.

The occupants seemed uninjured, the local policeman came running up, and the boys poured out of the shop to see the fun.

Tom and his pals were well to the fore, but directly Tom Shale saw the driver of the car he turned deathly pale. It was Slim Dolman, with another gangster beside him, and Nick Stiebel seated in the back of a heavy tourer.

Stiebel was arguing with the policeman, whilst his companion wasdoing the same with the lorry-driver.

Suddenly he looked up and saw Tom in front of him. The lad had not had time to withdraw. The gangster's eyes brightened. He pointed at Tom.

"That boy was close at the time. He'll be a witness for me. You can swear I was on my right side of the road, can't you?"

Tom's pals looked at him in surprise. Why had he been picked on like this?"

"Well, as a matter of fact—." he began cautiously, then got a fierce wink from Stiebel, "I think you were."

"There you are. You've got my name and address constable, and you can take this lad's name as well. I'm in a hurry. My friend and I have an appointment, and it's urgent. We—."

The constable barred his way with determination.

"No you don't. I'm sorry about this appointment, but you'd better phone and cancell it. You'r coming down to the station with me. This is a serious case. I saw you travelling at speed. You'll be charged with endangering the public, and unless you can produce bail—."

"Why you—," commenced Stiebel, then quickly subsided and grinned, "Okay! I'll come. We'll drive down in the car. She's only a bit dented. Jump in constable! Hey you! Don't forget what I said about being a witness."

It was Tom he beckoned to, and as the boy came close to the car something was deftly tossed towards him. It was done very quickly, but Tom Shale was not the best fielder in the cricket team for nothing. He caught the object by instinct, received another grin from Stiebel, and stepped back into the crowd.

His pals found him a moment later. But by that time he had been able to thrust into his pocket the rather bulky parcel which had been so surprisingly passed to him.

"You can't give evidence for that blighter," said Dick, "He was quite in the wrong. Wonder why he picked on you?"

Tom swollowed hard.

His hand was still in his pocket, and he was wondering what this packet contained. Obviously it was something Stiebel and his friends did not want taken to the police station in case the police saw it.

"Oh, he picked out the chap with the most intelligent face," he declared, and got a punch from his friends, "Let's go back and finish tea. I don't suppose I shall ever hear from him again."

Not until nearly an hour later, in the privacy of his own study, did he have a chance to open the package. The contents nearly knocked him backwards. It was a valuable necklace of the most perfect pearls Tom had ever seen. It must have been worth thousands of pounds.

In a flash he understood it all. The gang had robbed some house or person and Stiebel had been making off with the loot when the collison had occurred. The gangster must have considerd it to have his new chief near enough to be passed the necklace.

Tom hardly knew what to say or do. He closed the case hastily, and thrust it at the very back of the drawer with some books on top of it. Whose was it? He did not even know that. He had not even heard of a robbery in the district, yet here he was the reciever of stolen goods. Things were going from bad to worse.

Later that evening he made some excuse to visit the room of Mr Gable, the English master, and as he was about to leave he spied the late edition of the evening paper. He had only gone there because he remembered Mr Gable took it in.

"Excuse me sir, but may I glance at the sports news?" he asked picking up the newspaper.

"Cerainly Shale, take it along. I've finished with it."

Back in his room he eagerly searched the paper, and found what he wanted in the stop press at the back.

"Amazing daylight robbery," he read, "Motor bandits raid Wexburn Manor in early afternoon and make off with famous necklace."

The newspaper told how the bandits had driven up when only two servants were in the house and the owners were away in town. They had been masked and armed, the servants had been locked in a cupboard, and the raiders had got away with the pearl necklace, leaving no clue as to their identity. Nobody even rememdered seeing the car. A reward of five hundred pounds was offered for the return of the necklace.

And that was the necklace he had within a few feet of his hand, in his drawer!

The colour rushed to his face. Blind rage seized him. Why should he be made to meddle with all this crime and to be helpless to defend himself? Why should he mixed up in these beastly robberies and kidnappings?

He decided at once and for all to put a stop to it. He would pack up the necklace and post it back to the owners, telling the gang never to put such a thing in his way again. He would show them he wasn't afraid of them.

With the door locked, he made up a neat package. It was not very heavy, and he had enough stamps to stick on it. It was too late to catch the last collection from the school, but there was a postbox about one hundred yards down the road with a later collection. He could slip out and drop it in there.

The road seemed deserted, but his one fear was that he might meet some of the masters. One or two of them often took walks late in the evening.

But he reached the box without any trouble, and sighed with relief when he heard the package drop to the bottom of the box. At least that would be back at Wexburn Manor in the morning.

He grinned as he stuck his hands in his pockets and strode back towards the school on the hill. The gang would know better than to place stolen goods in his hands again. They might—.

"Hey chief. We were coming to look you up," came a quick growl from the shadows of a tree he was passing, "You've saved us the trouble."

Tom's heart nearly jumped through his mouth. It was Stiebel and another man, the one who had been with him in the car. They must have come across the field and just entered the road by way of the style.

"I'm in a hurry," said Tom, "I've got to get back, and I'm not supposed to be out at all."

Stiebel loomed alongside him, slender yet menacing.

"Then you'd better get that necklet and pass it to us as soon as possible. There's danger in keeping it. The Crawford bunch know we've got it, and I've seen two of them hanging around here."

Tom tried hard to keep cool.

"What do you mean about danger? Who's the Crawford gang?"

"Jake Crawford was your fther's chief rival. He used to try and butt in on our business. But this time we've put one over on him. He was after that necklet, and we got there first. He's got his crowd down here trying to get it back. If he hears you've got it he'll be after it like a shot. You'd better nip back and hand it over so's we can get it out of the country."

"But I haven't got it," cried Tom in mock dismay.

"Not got it! But you mean to say he's been clever enough to get it from you already?" almost howled Stiebel, "How on the—."

"Well," said Tom, "I don't know all the members of the gang by sight. When a stranger comes up to me and says I have to hand over the necklet to him. I naturally jump the conclusion that he's one of us. It went some time ago."

Stiebel leaned back heavily against the wall.

"The clever skunk. Then he knows all about you. This means he's already making for London. We've got to follow. It's our only chance. Six of the boys are down at the station. You'll come along to show us which man it was. Come on."

Almost before he knew it Tom was being rushed across the field to the lane on the other side, wher a big car awaited them.

His clever story was going to land him in more complications than he had expected.

PART THREE.

WHEN GANG MEETS GANG.

At the station, some two miles away, another car was waiting, with Slim Dolman and five others. In a few words Stiebel explained what he believed to have happened, and within five minutes Tom Shale found himself mixed up in an astounding adventure.

"Here's your chance. Chief," grinned Stiebel rather sarcastically, "This was the sort of job your father would have liked. See if you can't lead us as well as he would have done."

"Lead you, but I've got to be back at the school! If I'm missed—."

"Aw, forget that! We've missed something more important than that—the pearls. We've got to get them before Crawford and his bunch vanish in London. They'll be on the road now, and—Hi look!"

A big open topped car had just swung round from the village on to the London road, and the headlights of a car coming in the other direction had been for a moment directed on it. Nick Stiebel's eyes bulged with excitement.

"That's them! I saw Crawford sitting in the front. We're not too late after all. After them."

Tom was almost picked up and bundled into the first of the cars. Four other men scrambled in with him, and he felt something thrust into his hand. It was a revolver!

He nearly dropped the thing as though it was red hot. What was he doing chasing around the country with armed men and a gun in his fist? It seemed crazy.

But as the car jerked forward, with the second not far behind, the thrill of the chase entered his blood. After all, these ought to know their own enimies.

These were other gangster they were chasing, not law-abiding citizens. What was more, he had the laugh over them about the necklet, although they did not know it.

The two cars roared on through the night, but the tail-light in front seemed to get no nearer. Wether or not the Crawford men knew they were being pursued he could not tell, but they were hitting a dizzy speed.

Everyone sat forward with excitement, gripping their guns grimly. Few of the occupants of passing cars could even have climpsed them, they were travelling so fast.

The red tail-lights began to draw away from them. Nick Stiebel groaned.

"They've got a speedy bus. We can't do it. They'll be through Hounslow and into Londonbefore we have a chance."

Tom Shale leaned over and tapped the driver excitedly.

"Hi, there's a road down to the right over the bridge. It's a very bad surface and there is a water splash halfway, but it cuts off a couple of miles before it rejoins the road. We use it for our annual cross-country. You ought to be able to get through."

The gangsters eagerly took the advice. They were willing to take any risks, to try anything at all, in order to get at those they believe to have stolen their loot. They shrieked for the driver to make the attempt, and he was able to slow down in time.

By this time Tom had forgotten everything except the thrill of the chase. He had forgotten who he was with, and all about school.

Crash! Bump! He had certainly been right when he had warned them about the roughness of the going. Cars rarely came through here because of the water-splash, there being a wide stream without any bridges.

Crash! Bump! They were thrown one against the other, tossed from side to side, and their heads thumped on the roof of the saloon. But the driver managed to keep her right way up, and a few minutes later there came a terrific rush of water over and around the windscreen.

Splash! There came one dreadful moment when it seemed that the car must stop.

The driver had taken the water-splash too fast, but thanks to the fine driving they went through and up the other side.

Now they could see the lights of the main road ahead, and Tom wondered what they were going to do. He soon knew.

The driver swerved to the left towards London, swung his car broadside across the road and deliberatly stopped. Tom and the others immediately jumped out. Up the hill beyond came the whine of a powerful car driven hard in second gear.

"That's them! I recognise the note."

The gangsters stood at either end of the car, clear of the centre of the road. It was not the first time they had stopped a car in this manner.

Tom began to get worried. It looked to him as though he had made it possible for a disaster to occur on the main London road that night. Then he remembered that it was only a gang war. The more of both sides who got hurt the better for law-abiding citizens.

On came the car over he brow of the hill,but the driver saw the obstacle in time.

His brakes squealed as he swerved, but there was no room for him to pass at either end. He was forced to a stop, and as he came to rest a volley of shots rang out from the Grizzlies.

They were firing not at the car, but at the tyres. They seemed to have hit their mark, for the sound of bursting tubes added to the general din.

Ping! A shot passed Tom's ear. Someone in Crawford's carwas shooting to kill. He forgot all the gun in his fist. He only knew he might have been killed, and he ws very angry.

The man was leaning over the side to take aim at one of the others when Tom's big fist crashed alongside his ear. He sprawled sideways, and the door came suddenly open, sending him into the roadway. Tom kicked his gun under the car.

There were only four men in the machine which had been held up, and there were eight of the Grizzlies not counting Tom. With their leader sprawled in the road the other three quickly made up their minds to surrender.

They were dragged out and disarmed.

Dolman found time to give Tom a slap on the back.

"That was fine the way you punched Crawford's jaw! Your a real chip of the old block."

But the Grizzlies were anxious to get off the main road, where at any moment other traffic might arrive. They grabbed their prisoners and ran them into a field, where there were some trees which gave them cover.

Two of their number stayed behind to search their car for the missing necklet. Tom began to wonder what would happen next. How long would it be before they discovered his story was a bluff? What would they do to him when they did discover this?

Crawford and his three men were dragged amonst the trees and spreadeagled on the ground. Crawford was groaning, the others were looking sullen.

Nick Stiebel levelled his gun at Crawford, who was a fat man with narrow eyes and a loose mouth.

"Come across with it, Crawford, come across!"

"Don't know what your snarling about," growled the other, "You'll pay for this."

"Don't try to bluff. We want the Wexburn necklet, and quick."

"What!" the other's eyes widened, "Are you plum crazy? You"ve got the necklet, and we were trying—."

"Bah! Don't try to bluff, unless you want one of these bullets in your teeth. We had the necklet, that's true, but you've got it from one of us by a trick. If you haven't got it here you know where it is, and unless you tell us mighty quick we're going to shoot. Make up your mind."

"But I tell you—." began Crawford pale with terror.

Stiebel gave him a vicious kick in the ribs.

"Blakey, where are you? Where's Blakey?"

One of the Grizzlies, an unpleasant-looking brute, came eagerly forward, "You know how to stir up a man's nerves with a knife. Get busy on Crawford, and make him talk. Don't forget the quicker we get away from here the better. Those shots may have been heard."

Blakey dropped on one knee beside the squirming Crawfod, who was being held by two of the Grizzlies. Crawford began to gasp and beg for mercy, for he knew he was going to be tortured.

Tom Shale, standing by, felt his mouth go dry with horror. He could not let a man be tortured for something he had done himself.

He lifted his revolver to theaten them, then thought of a better way. He turned and flashed a shot into the darkness, the first time he had ever fired a heavy weapon .

"Quickly! The police!" he roared.

Instantly there was mad confusion, Blakey and the others leap to their feet, released the prisoner, and ran for their lives. They scattered in all directions. Crawford and his men manages to rise as well. They had no more wish to be captured by the police than their rivals. They bolted through the woods like rabbits.

Only Tom Shale was left standing on the scene of the hold-up, and he had a broad grin on his face when he turned back towards the roadway.

"That's done the trick anyhow!"

But he was still on the far side of the hedge from the roadway when a fast-driven car drew up alongside the gangster's car on the road.

"Here's the place! It's been a hold-up. I knew it was shots and not backfiring we heard," snapped a voice, "Look! There's a gap in the hedge."

Two men crashed just past Tom Shale as he flattened himself in the darkness. Both were in the uniform of the police. They were two of the mobile patrol. Tom had not been far wrong when he had faked that alarm to help Crawford.

CHAPTER THREE.

PART ONE.

TOM SHALE IN THE SOUP.

St Ardens school was in darkness, which was not surprising, considering it was three o'clock in the morning, but somehow Tom Shale did not like the look of things. Everything was too quiet.

The captain of St Ardens was plastered in mud, his clothing was tornin several places, and there was a streak of blood on his face where a bramble had caught him. He had come a long wayacross country, and he was tired. He wanted nothing better than to be in bed.

He knew the right spot to shin up over the wall and drop into the quad. He drew a deep breath and made for the end of the building. There was his window, partly open as usual, and no more than fifteen feet up, but that fifteen feet wanted some climbing. How was he going to get up?

He had left the school shortly before ten o'clock the previous evening to visit the post box down the road. He knewhe had been breaking all the rules by going out of bounds like this, but the matter was urgent.

What had happened since then was a;lmost a nightmare. There was a bulge in his pocket which was a reolver. He had fired it once and had no intention of doing so again. For the moment he was wondering how he was to reach his room without arousing anyone.

It would be a terribly serious matter for him is he was caught. The captain of the school was supposed to set an example to the others in all things, and up till now there had been no more dutiful captain than Tom Shale. But eveything had changed when his father had died. It had been the biggest shock of his life to discover that his father, Captain Shale, had been no other than the notorious, Scarface Shale, the leader of a gang of crooks.

It seemed almost unbelievable, but the gang had not only proved this to Tom, but had insisted that he should take over his father's place and lead them, so that there would be no quarrelling.

it had all seemed crazy. How could a boy at school lead a crooked gang? But events had followed thick and fast, they had threatened him with death, and his father's name with exposure. In self-defence he had been forced to pretend to agree, and already they had got him mixed up in crime.

On each occasion he had tricked them without them knowing it, and that very night he had bluffed them into fighting with a rival gang over a pearl necklace they had stolen. Thanks to Tom, the necklace was already on it's way back to it's rightful owner.

He remembered how when he had been a younger boy he had several times entered the school by a tree which grew near Dormitory D. He walked round there and looked up at it.

Yes, it was still possible. Only the previous he had swished one of the Fourth for sneaking out after dark. The boy must have used the same tree.

It meant passing through the Fourth Form dormitory, but there was no other way, and already the cockerals in the nearby farms were crowing. Daylight was not very far off.

The tree creaked beneath his weight, but he discovered his greater reach made it easier for him to climb than before. He edged out along the one strong branch, which bent beneath his weight, reached over, and got a grip on the window sill.

There he was, dangling by his hands, and he knew that, whatever happened, he would have to go through with it. To go back was impossible, to drop was to risk a broken leg.

He hauled himself up and cautiously peered through the window, which by a rule of school was left wide open. Tom heard the sound of regular deep breathing. There were thirty boys in there, and if one spotted him it would be all up.

Silently he wriggled over the sill, and dropped inside. He had already taken off his boots and tied them round his neck by the laces. His feet made no sound.

Rows of beds on both sides. He tiptoed down the middle, his heart pounding loudly.

Everything seemed alright. He was within a yard of the door, and thinking of reaching for the door knob, whena shrill voice from one of the beds queried—.

"Who's that?"

It was young Perkins, one of the sharpest youngsters in the school. The captain of St Ardens decided on a real bluff.

He whirled towards the bed.

"Was it you I heard out of bed just now, Perkins? What were you up to?"

"N-no, I-I only just woke up and saw you there," protested Perkins, "I thought it was a burgler."

"If I find out who's been prowling about I'll give him the licking of a lifetime," promised the captain, confident that nothing of his appearance could be seen in the darkness.

"Go to sleep and don't let me hear another sound."

With that he walked out of the doorway. In the corridor beyond he could not resist a grin. That was sheer bluff, but he believed it had worked.

Along one corridor, down some stairs, and up some others on the far side of the hall. He met nobody on the way, and reached his own little room with a sigh of relief.

He opened the door quietly, closed it again before switching on the light, and then turned with a startled gasp.

He was not alone in the room. Sitting in the chair beside his unruffled bed was Dr Lumley, the Headmaster himself.

Tom Shale felt like sinking through the floor. Nothing that had happened to him that night had scared him like this. The Doctor's face was bleak and hard. He rose swiftly.

"Well, so you've come back at last, Shale. I thought maybe you were making a night of it."

Tom could only open and shut his mouth like a landed fish. What was the use of saying anything when he was in that state, with his boots around his neck?

I—I—."

"I suppose you are going to explain where you, the captain of the school, have been? Well?"

Tom cleared his throat.

"I'm sorry sir, but I can't do that. It was private business of my own, and I was—was detained. I had only intended going out to post a letter."

"Ah! That's why you were not in your room when I came to discuss the new

Second Eleven just after ten," snapped the Head, "Private business! A nice thing when the captain of my school sneaks out at the dead of night on private business. Is that all you have to say for youself?"

He was taking in every detail of the lad's appearance, the mud, and the scratches.

"Have you been fighting?" he demanded.

"No—er—yes, sir. I was forced into it!" stammered Tom, "But I can assure you, sir, that it was nothing dishonourable. I did nothing to shame the school. It was forced on me."

Dr Lumley looked at him keenly.

They always had a good respect for each other, and now he saw the agony in the boy's eyes. There must be something behind it all.

"Can't you tell me, Shale?" he asked more kindly.

Tom bit his lips.

That was the last thing he dared do. He had not even told his best pals a word about the amazing thing which had happened to him. How could he tell the Headmaster that his father had been a master crook and that he was now being forced to lead those same gangsters. It would sound too fantastic and impossible.

So, Tom tightened his lips.

"I'm afraid not, sir."

"Well, Shale, I suppose I ought to look for a new captain, but that would mean a big scandal in the school, and would do us no good. I cannot trust you in the future as I have done in the past, but I still believe you have the honour of the school at heart."

"Yes, sir, I have. I woundn't do a thing—."

"Yet you broke out of bounds in this amazing manner and came back here in this state. You have risked discovery by any boy in the school. Has any other person here seen or guessed what you have done?"

"No, ir, I'm sure of that?"

The Doctor sighed with relief. In his heart he was very fond of big Tom Shale.

"Very well, then I shall deal with the matter privately between us. You will take a thrashing from me alone, then you will give me your word of honour that nothing loke this will ever happen again. In consideration of that I will say no more about the matter."

Tom's lips worked without a sound coming from them. He did not mind the licking so much, although he knew that in the Doctor's present mood it would be a severe one, but how could he give his word that it would not happen again? The gang would put pressure on him, would make demands which they would force him to comply with. It was not fair. He was dragged in two directions at once.

"Of course I'll take the caning, sir, but as regards the promise—."

"I shall flog you until you give me that promise!" snapped Dr Lumley, losing his temper, "I am going to my study to wait for you. Get out of those filthy clothes and into some pjamas. I'll attend to you at once."

Tom bit his teeth together hard. It looked as though he was in for a hard time. The Doctor meant to force the promise from him.

"Very well, sir, I'll be there in five minutes."

The Doctor went away, and Tom changed.

He got into pjamas and dressing gown, then left the room feeling like a prisoner leaving the condemned cell on the way to the scaffold. Only once in the history of the school had the Doctor caned a Sixth Form boy, and that had been an event to talk about. He knew he was due for the licking of his life, and all because he had been mixed up in the Wexburn necklace affair.

The Doctor's study was at the end of a corridor away from the dormitories. A faint grey light was just coming in through the window as Tom neared the door and tapped.

"Come in!" growled Dr Lumley, and Tom Shale felt his knees shaking as they had never done since he had been in the Third.

PART TWO.

THE GRIZZLIES STOP A LICKING.

The blinds were up, and there was only that grey light in the room. Dr Lumley looked tired and drawn, but he would not be too tired to use that cane he waved in such a business-like manner.

"Well, Shale, take off that dressing gown and get over the end of the settee. To thrash a boy of your age and intelligence hurts me as much as it will hurt you, but you deserve all you are going to get."

Tom's face was crimson as he bent over the end of the leather settee, which had been the foundation for so many canings at St Ardens. He had never expected to have to go through this in his life again.

It was ridiculousthat it should happen to him, and only a few hours earlier he had been battling with the Grizzlies against their enemies, the Crawford Gang.

He heard the Doctor lift the cane, waited for the swish with clenched hands, then nearly rolled from the settee in amazement when there came a crash of glass behind him.

Had the Doctor knocked something off the desk with the cane? He half-turned his head, saw that it was the lower part of the window that was smashed, and gulped when he noticed a hand levelling a revolver was protruded through the broken window.

"Stop that! Let the kid get up!" snarled a harsh voice, and Tom Shale felt that he really must be dreaming, for that was the voice of Slim Dolman, one of the Grizzlies.

The cane dropped to the Doctor's side. The gangster coolly reached in with his other hand, pushed over the window catch, and opened it.

"One cheep out of either of you and I shoot!" he growled.

Dr Lumley found his wits returning along with his voice.

"What does this mean? Who are you? Get out of here before I call the police."

"No you don't!" Slim Dolman was into the room and standing before the telephone in a flash. Outside the window were two more of the gang.

"We mean business. We're the gang who tried to kidnapp the American kid the other week. That failed. Now we're after this boy here. Shale's his name isn't it?"

"Yes, but—."

"What's in that cupboard?" snapped Dolman, suddenly jerking his gun towards a corner.

"Maps only, but—"

Dr Lumley hardly knew whether he was on his feet or his head.

"Then get back in there. Quickly!"

The barrel of the gun against his chest forced the Headmaster of St Ardens into the corner. A few moments later he was wedged amongst the maps, and Slim Dolman was locking the door from the outside.

"One word outa you for the next half-hour and it'll be your last."

He turned to the gaping Tom and favoured him with a wink and a grin. Then in a harsh voice he commanded.

"You put on that dressing-gown and get through the window! Jump to it!"

"But—." protested Tom.

"I said out through that window," roared Dolman, and at the same time made frantic motions towards the cupboard, "Are the others to come and carry you out after I've hit you on the head? Take that!"

He kicked the desk most artistically. From within the cupboard came the sound of a groan. Dr Lumley thought Tom was being knocked about.

The boy sighed as he put on his gown.

It seemed that there was to be no bed for him that night. He got out through the window, and was immediately grabbed by either arm and rushed to the side gate from the quad to the lane. Outside was a waiting car, and he was inside this almost before he started to speak.

"Look here—," he protested.

"Well, chief, wasn't it a good thing we turned up when we did?" said Dolman, sinking into the cushions beside him, "We just came to make sure you'd got back safely, and we found the old man about to lick the stuffing out of you. Reckon we did you a good turn."

"I'd sooner have taken the licking!" roared Tom Shale, "What's going to be the result of this? I shall only get into a worse mess than before, and—."

"Nix on that! That's why we pretended to kidnap you. We'll let you go later in the morning, and then you can make a wonderful escape and return to the school. They'll all be so pleased to see you safe and sound that he'll forget all about the licking and the other trouble."

"It would have been better if we'd bumped that old Doc off!" growled one of the others.

Tom shuddered.

These were the sort of men he was forced to mix with, and who considered themselves as friends.

They wrapped a motor rug round him, and to change the subject he asked—.

"What happened after we scattered? Did the police get anyone?"

"Nobody. There were only two of them, after all, but Crawford and his boys escaped in the scrimmage, and with them went our chance of getting back the necklace. We're real sorry that happened, chief. It wasn't our fault. We didn't know they were already in the neighbourhood."

Tom felt nearer grinning than he had for some time. Here they were apologising to him for having lost the nacklace, and it was him who posted it back to the owner.

"We won't forget this," he said as harshly as he could, "Crawford must be taught a lesson."

There were growls of approval. In his heart he hoped that if the gangs got busy fighting each other there would be less time for them to trouble law-abiding folk.

The car sped on through the grey dawn, finally turning into the drive of a big country house which Tom had known as empty for some time. The agents' boards were still up, offering it for sale, but it was no longer empty, as the Grizzlies were using it for their headquarters. As it was buried amonst the trees there was little fear of anyone seeing them or watching their comings and goings.

Most of the gang had returned there, and messages had been promised from those who had gone on towards London to try and discover what had happened to the Crawford gang.

For the next ten minutes they talked of the night's events, but Tom was so sleepy that he blinked as he tried to follow their conversation. The chief thing was that they did not suspect for one moment that their new leader had cheated them out of the necklace they had stolen. They would have lynched him if they had guessed this.

Seeing his yawns, Dolman suggested that he should sleep, and a few minutes later he was snoring on a settee in another room.

How long he slept he did not know, but he was aroused by one of the gang with a cup of tea. The sun was shining through the windows, and it seemed to be about noon.

"Drink this chief. Dolman says it's nearly time for you to escape."

Tom drank, and was much refreshed. The events of the night came back to him, and his kidnapping by the gang. Presently Dolman appeared, and they talked things over.

It was finally decided to drop Tom about a mile from the school, and he was to make his way back across country, telling on his arrival some story of having been tied to a tree in a copse all night, and finally breaking his bonds and getting clear.

"They'll make a hero out of you, chief," grinned Dolman, "I'll bet to one the old Doc don't say no more about that licking."

Tom did not take the bet.

He felt rather ashamed of himself for the trick he was going to play on everyone at school, but it was the only way he could get out of things.

The gang gave him breakfast, and just before he was due to leave Nick Stiebel arrived with the news that they had lost the Crawford gang.

"But don't you worry, Chief," he said, "We'll get 'em sooner or later. They won't be allowed to get at you again. Some of us will be right here in this house. If we want you we'll send for you."

Tom's fists clenched.

"I can't come at night again. The Doc will watch me like a cat watching a mouse after this."

Nick Stiebel smiled his unpleasant grin. Of them all he was the one Tom disliked most.

"Don't you worry about that, Chief. We'll settle the Doc when the time comes. We know how to take care of ourselves, and you too."

With that far from comforting assurance they sent Tom out in the car with two of the gang, who took him by byways and lanes to a chosen spot in sight of the school.

He was still wearing pyjamas and dressing-gown, it was lucky it was a warm day, for he knew that for the time he had climbed through a few hedges there would be very little of either left. His arrival at St Ardens would hardly be a dignified one.

The car departed.

Tom commenced his painful journey, and just before afternoon lessons began the school was thrilled with the news of his return.

Rumours spread wildly.

He had battled his way out single-handed and run ten miles across country, said somebody

he had been saved because someone had paid ransom for him, said another imaginative person. Nobody knew the truth.

As a matter of fact, Tom told his story very simply to the Doctor and the dectives, who had at once come to St Ardens to investigate this second case of kidnapping. He had talked everything over with Dolman, so he made no slips. When he had finished it was the Doctors who put an arm round him and led him to his room.

"Thank goodness you are safe, Shale. Now you need a hot bath and then twenty-fours in bed. I'll see that your meals are sent to you. Now I must hurry away and try and hush all this up, or the world will begin to thinkthat kidnapping is a part of our regular programmes at St Arden.

In bed between clean sheets, Tom Shale could not help chuckling to himself.

"Dolman was right," he thought, "The Doc's forgotten all about the other matter and the swishing he promised me.

The Grizzlies centainly had brains.

PART THREE.

CIRCUS NIGHT.

Two weeks had passed, and Tom Shale had not heard a single word from the Grizzlies. The excitement about his kidnapping had died down, although there was still a special police patrol round the school at nights.

He wondered wether it was this patrol which prevented the gang from communicating with him, and hoped so. But, on the other hand, it might mean they were busy with their gang battle with Crawford. In any case, he hoped he was free from the nightmare, which had come into his life, and he threw himself heart and soul into the opening of the football season.

St Ardens had always had a very strong football team, but this year they hoped to put out a second eleven which would be nearly as good as the first. It meant a good deal of practice, of selection, coaching and arranging. Tom Shale found himself too busy to worry much about the gangsters.

   The weather was dry and crisp. The nights had not yet got too short, and they were able to have some practice nearly every afternoon before prep.

   Tom usually played with the chosen youngsters in order to see how they really were, and he was in football gear this afternoon when a sudden rainstorm drove them all to cover

   many of the youngsters changed in the pavilion. Tom had his raincoat, and he decided to sprint back to the school and have a proper bath and a rub down before dressing.

   It was coming down cats and dogs, but he was already as wet as could be, and did not mind very much. Head down, he tore along the muddy road, thinking of little beyond the prospects of a warm bath.

   As he passed the field at the corner of the bridge from the town he noticed a circus had erected it's tents there. Big bills had been stuck up, advertising all sorts of marvels which were to be shown.

   It was really a first class show of it's kind, and was expected to draw thousands, as there had not been one for a very long time.

   Most of the boys from the school had bought tickets. Dr Lumley had granted special permission for them to attend an evening performance that very day.

   "The field will turn into a quagmire if this rain lasts," thought Tom, "A good thing the tent is already up, or—."

   Bump!

   Something had bounced right before him in the road, splashing him with mud. He turned and stared after it, it was a football, and for the moment he expected to see the boy who had kicked it. It was a strick rule for the schoolboys that footballs were not to be kicked about the streets.

   There would be serious trouble if the owner was found, for Tom took it for granted that it was one from the school.

   He picked it up and carried it grimly under his arm.

"If they want it, they'll jolly well have to come for it!" he muttered, "Then I'll have something to say about kicking footballs in the lanes."

A few moments later he was returning the brief salute of one of the constables who now patrolled the district round the school. It was comforting to see them there. If the gang could not communicate with him he could not be expected to go to them or take part in any of their crimes.

He dumped the football in his room, had a bath, and a brisk rub-down, then did not think of the ball again until he was fully dressed.

By that time it had dried, and he wiped it to try and see some identification mark on it.

"Wonder if it does belong to the school, or whether one of the townies kicked it over the hedge? If they'd done it why didn't they come out for it afterwards? It's strange."

Then he remembered that initials and names were sometimes marked on the inner bladder, which did not get the rough treatment that the outer case did. He untied the string, and let down the ball, opening the laces to remove the bladder.

Then his eyes bulged. Out from between the bladder and the lether covering fell a sheet of white paper, crumpled but clean and fresh. As one in a daze he picked it up and read—.

"To the chief,—. There is a big job on tonight. We are holding up the circus and cleaning it out. The gang will be there in full force. Do not fail us. If necessary get special permission from the Doc to attend a performance. We may need your help, —. The Grizzlies."

There was really no need for that signature. The first words had told him the worst. The Grizzlies had found a way of communicating with him after all, and their plan for the evening horrified him.

There would be at least two thousand people there, and the takings would probably be somewhere between four and five hundred pounds. In addition, there would be money and valuables. It would make a rich haul for determined men like the Grizzlies. No wonder they had thought of making the attempt.

But Tom Shale had not become captain of St Ardens without being a bright lad. His firm jaw crept out, his hands clenched. The gang thought it was going to bring him in on this, and to make him take part in it.

He paced his study doing some hard thinking.

By the time the rest of the boys had returned from the football ground he had decided, and there was a glint in his eyes which warned his friends to keep away from him.

"What's the matter with Tom?" pondered Dick Seymour, his best pal, "He looks on the warpath about something. Hello, Tom, going to the circus tonight?"

"Yes, I've got a ticket," acknowledged the captain, "There'll be a terrific crush there. I'm going early."

"I'll come along as well, so will Reddy Trotter," said his friend, and there was no hope of refusing their company wiyhout rousing their suspicions.

The performance was due to begin at eight o'clock, and it was only just after seven when the three senior boy found their way down to the fairground. There was all kinds of sideshows and attractions besides the circus, and a large crowd had already collected.

They tried their luck with the coconuts until Reddy Trotter, who was the fastest bowler in the school, knocked off so many that the man refused to sell them anymore balls.

The crowd increased, and it was as they pressed closed to the shooting-gallery that someone nudged Tom. Looking up quickly, he found himself gazing into the smiling face of Slim Dolman. The man winked at him, then vanished in the throng.

Not a dozen paces on someone whispered—.

"Hello, chief."

Turning his head sharply, Tom Shale noticed Nick Stiebel's ugly face turned in his direction. The Grizzlies were already there in full force. They meant mischief, and it was easy what an opportunity they would have amonst such a crowd as this.

Tom's hands clenched tighter.

The man at the circus was banging the drum and inviting all and sundry to walk up. Tom's two friends were all for going up and getting a front seat.

Tom had been carrying his cap in his hand to let the evening air cool his forehead. Now he deliberatly dropped his cap, and a few minutes later cried,—.

"Hang on a few minutes you chaps! I've dropped my cap. I think I know where it happened. I'll slip back for it."

He had darted through the crowd before hos pals could say a word, but he did not go towards his cap. Instead, he turned between the big stationary traction engines which were making the electric current, dodged round behind some caravans, and reached the back of the circus.

There he had already seen the covered cages and pens where the performing animals were kept. One or two attendants were about, but most of them were called to work in the "big top" as the circus folk called the large tent where the show was given.

Tom looked up and down the rows of cages. Most of the beasts looked weary and half-starved. Some were yawning with boredom, for they knew their performance in the ring was near at hand, and they were fed up with the idea.

Tom selected an old lioness in a cage. She had her eyes closed until Tom was standing right alongside the cage, and then she opened her eyes and mouth at the same time to yawn. He looked right down the vast throat and realised that she had no teeth. There was no wonder the performers in the ring did not mind taking chances with her.

She was just what Tom Shale wanted.

He clanced right and left to make sure he was not being watched, and then reached in and unlatched the door.

The door did not open until he pulled it, and even then the lioness did not rise.

"Come on out. It's your big chance!" he growled, but thelioness said and did nothing.

Tom was impatient. He picked up a pole and poked the lioness, then wished he had not, for with remarkable agility she turned on the pole, knocked it from his hand with one swish of it's fore-paw, and leapt past him into the open.

A moment latershe was rummaging about amonst the garbage beneath the cages, sniffing her way lazily towards the open fair ground.

Tom hurled down the pole and filled his lungs.

"Lion escaped!" he bellowed, "Lion loose! Run for your lives! A lion is loose!"

The lioness turned and blinked at him, wondering why all the noise was being made.

Then she ambled off amonst the dense crowd outside and in a moment there was the wildest uproar all over the fairground.

"Lion escaped! Run for your lives!"

CHAPTER FOUR.

PART ONE.

BIG CHIEF TOM SHALE.

Two thousand people stampeding in all directions, two thousand people yelling in terror! It was an awesome sight, but Tom Shale was glad of it.

As he ducked between the traction engines which still churned out the power and light for the circus, his eyes were bright with satisfaction, for the riot was of his making. It was he who had released the old lioness which had innocently caused the panic, and he who had raised the first shout of—.

"Lion escaped! Lion loose! Run for your lives!"

Now he saw the circus hands crowding to the spot, desperately striving to steady the crowd and herd them back towards the big tent. The circus men themselves could not imagine what had happened, but they knew very well that none of their animals were dangerous, and they were trying to tell the crowd so.

They might just as well have tried to stop the tide from coming in. they were nearly knocked over by the rush of people for the exits. A few were trampled, stalls were knocked over and their contents spilled, but Tom Shale, the captain of St Ardens, was still not sorry for what he had done.

When Tom Shale had released the lioness he had not meant it for a schoolboy jape. He was old enough to know better. He had been made to do so for a far stronger reson.

On the circus ground that night was a gang of crooks known as the Grizzlies, and their intention had been to wait until the circus show was in full swing, with nearly two thousand people in the tent, then stage a hold-up. They had meant to rake in thousands of pounds that night, and there would probably have been shooting and killing if anyone had resisted, for the Grizzlies stuck at nothing.

Tom Shale knew all about this forthcoming attempt for the simple reason that he was the leader of the Grizzlies!

It was an amazing situation in which the popular captain of St Ardens found himself. Captain Thomas Shale, his father, had always been something of a mystery, and had always spent long periods on the continent on business. But not until he had died did Tom learn the frightful truth.

His father was "Scareface" Shale, the leader of this gang of crooks, and he had died during a fight with the police. The gang had come to England and told Tom the truth, and as there was some argument amonst them as to who should be the new leader, they decided to settle the matter by making their late leader's son his successor.

In vain had Tom refused and protested. They had pointed out that if he refused they would not only brand his father as a crook in the eyes of the whole world, but would slay Tom ass well.

Then the captain of St Ardens had made up his mind, and he had promised himself that, although he might have to pretend to be their leader, he would use them merely for his own ends, and would cut in on their plans at every move.

Learning of the intended hold-up at the circus, and having been asked to be there by the Grizzlies, he had chosen this means of upsetting their plans. There could be no hold-up if the audience departed hurriedly! It was bettter to have a little damage done in this way than tragedy and great loss of money through the hold-up.

He saw his two pals, Dick Seymour and Reddy Trotter, standing just where he had left them. They were looking anxious, for he had pretended to be going back for his cap.

Dick seized his arm.

"We wondered whether the lion had got you, Tom. What a riot! Wonder how much truth there is in it?"

"Something escaped right enough," growled Tom, "I saw a lion loose over there. One of the cages must have come undone."

Reddy's eye glistened. Far from being afraid, the St Ardens boys were rather thrilled.

"What a lark! Wish I had my air-pistol here!"

Crack! Crack! The unmistakable sound of shots came from behind the cages. Tom's fists clenched.

"That wasn't an air-pistol, but a real revolver. Maybe the circus men are shooting the runaway."

He felt quite sorry for the lioness, but in any case it's life in that cage must have been a hideous one. In his heart, however, Tom was wondering whether it was a circus man who was shooting or one of the Grizzlies.

Someone grabbed his arm as they shouldered their way past.

"What rotten luck!" snarled the man, and Tom was in time to recognise Nick Stiebel, one of the ugliest of the Grizzlies. The gangster looked livid with rage.

Dick's ears were keen. He looked after Steibel curiously.

"What did he say, Tom? Why did he speak to you?"

Tom Shale shrugged his shoulders.

"Search me! He said something about it being rotten luck. Maybe he's one of the circus men grumbling at the big gate they've lost tonight. Come on, you chaps, we ought to see how some of the juniors are getting on."

There were over a hundred of the St Ardens boys there that evening. Special permission had been received for them to attend, and now the three seniors along with one of the masters, raised the school rally call, and ordered everyone to fall in on the road clear of the stampeding crowd.

Scores of the boys obeyed orders, but there was still a lot missing. Some of them did not intend to return to school until they had seen the last of the "fun". Tom found a couple of the younger ones hiding under a caravan, and yanked them out by their ears.

"You fall in, or there'll be all the trouble you want when you get back to school."

By this time the hands had discovered tht the only animal to escape was the old lioness, which someone had mysteriously shot. They were using megaphones to tell the crowdthat the performance would be taking place as usual, but the audience was not returning. They had been too scared to think of sitting down and watching the animals go through their paces. Police had arrived on the scene, and the riot was now under control, but the Chief Constable advised that there should be no attempt to hold the show.

There was now only three of the St Ardens boys missing. Two more of the masters had arrived from the school on hearing of the trouble, and now they helped the prefects in their search for the missing three.

Most of the lights had been put out, but here and there by flares the moody circus hands were repairing damage or righting overturned stalls. On all sides were groans and curses about the big crowd they had lost that night, but Tom reflected grimly that they would have been even more sorry for themselves if they had been robbed of every penny on the ground, and maybe some of them shot as well.

He found one of the boys interestingly watching what was going on, and chased him back to the fold. On the far side of the big circus tent he almost collided with a man, who at once seized his arm.

"Chief! We wondered what had happened to you."

It was Slim Dolman, another of the Grizzlies, and like Stiebel, he looked savagely disappointed.

Tom gave him no chance to say what he was going to say. The boy took the words out of his mouth.

"What rotten luck! How did this stampede start? How did that lion get loose?"

"Beats me, chief! The boys were all set. Everything was ready, and we'd have made a rare clean-up. Then this had to happen."

Tom looked as fierce as possible. Of late he had learned how to play his part.

"Are we never going to have any good luck? Ever since I've led you fellows things have gone wrong. You've not pulled off one single stunt without trouble. I'm beginning to think that your a crowd of bungling amateurs."

Another of the Grizzlieshad come up, and was standing listening respectfully. Tom gave them a rare tongue-lashing. Having made certain that their plot had failed, he proceeded to put the blame on them. He made them wince by calling them softies and bunglers. Slim Dolman began to look quite sorry for himself.

"What you say is right enough, chief, but I thought—we thought—you wouldn't be so keen on this sort of thing as you are. Some of the boys even said we were crazy to trust you, and that you'd sell us. But I can see they're wrong. Your a real chip of the old block. We'll take good care things don't go wrong the next time we take a job on hand, chief."

Tom's lips were twitching.

He was going to take jolly good care things did go wrong if he could manage it. He knew he was playing a very dangerous game, double-crossing this gang as he was doing, but he was beginning to enjoy himself.

"Well you can tell the rest of the gang from me that I'm fed up with there being trouble every time they take on a job," he growled, "Tell them I'll expect better results next time."

"Yes, chief, I will. Maybe it won't be worth while us trying the same circus racket again, but we'll think of something else. The Westbourne races come off next week, and Stiebel has got the idea of—."

"Shale! What are you wasting time talking there for?" rasped a voice, and Tom turned to see Mr Raft, the history master, looming over him, "You were to rake in the other boys, not to spend time gossiping. We've got everyone now, and your holding us up."

Tom suddenly felt very small. One moment he had been tricking and bossing a gang of grown men, the next he was ticked off like any other schoolboy by his master.

"Sorry, sir, I—er—didn't notice the time."

He turned his back on the two gangsters and followed Mr Raft, who was snorting indignantly.

"And who was those two undesirable-looking characters, Shale? I was surprised to see you talking to them."

Tom thought grimly that Mr Raft would have been shocked and surprised by a lot of things if he could only have known, but he answered meekly enough.

"Just two of the men here, sir. I was talking to them about the riot, and they said only one lion had escaped. It was quite harmless, and wouldn't hurt a fly. Funny how these things start, isn't it, sir?"

The history master that it was very funny, and then they hadrejoined the others.

The march back to school began.

PART TWO.

USELESS MONEY.

Life settled down to it's humdrum routine at St Ardens for all except Tom Shale. There was no possibility of thing being humdrum to him, when at any moment of the day or night he was liable to receive word from the Grizzlies that would dump him into the midst of crimes and alarms.

It was a nerve-racking position to be in, but luckily Tom was made of stern stuff, and he managed not only to attend to his work, but to take his usual interest in the football season, which was now in full stride.

With the nights drawing in so fast, there was not much time to waste, and a spell of hard, dry weather made it possible for the teams to get all the practice they wanted.

A week passed without hearing anything from the gang, and he wondered if they had gone off somewhere else to try and justify themselves in his eyes. He believed he had stung their pride by ticking them off as he had done, many times he chuckled over it. If they ever discovered he was the one responsible for their recent failures, death could the least he could expect.

Then one morning a registered letter came for him, and something made him keep it unopened until he was in the safety of his own den. There he got the shock of his life, for when he had removed the double covering he found no less than twenty ten pound notes.

There was also a scribbled letter;

"Dear Chief, it said, "We've just got back from Amsterdam. We didn't do badly over a diamond deal there, and this two hundred quid represents your usual tenth share. Might keep you in pocket-money until we pull off the scoop at the races next week."

There was no signature, but there did not need to be. Tom knew perfectly who the note and the money was from. So the Grizzlies had been up to mischief again, and had made two thousand pounds by some deal. He could guess the kind of "deal" it would have been. That represented the leader's share one-tenth of the whole.

His fingers crumpled the crisp notes. He had never had so much money in all his life. What could he do with it? He could not possibly keep stolen money, for such it undoubtedly was. If the Grizzlies had made a profit it would not have been an honest one. They had been up to some game, and if he accepted the money he would lower himself to their level.

So occupied was he with his thoughts that he did not hear a slight tap on the door behind him or see it immediately pushed open by a tall thin boy, whose eyes were watery behind his spectacles.

Jeff Barber, one of the Fifth Form boys, had a habit of walking like a cat, and he had never showed his gifts in this direction to greater advantage than now. Barber had no idea of creeping in upon the school captain in this manner. He just could not help it, but as soon as he saw the bundle of notes spread in Tom's hand his heart almost stopped beating. He stepped back and closed the door except for one inch.

Jeff Barber was a queer lad. He had no friends in his Form. Nobody liked him, for they considered him a sneak and a rotter. Even now he had been on his way to tell some sneaking tale to Tom. Sight of that money had changed his ideas. He remained there as silently as a mouse, his mouth watering.

He saw Tom shrug his shoulders, shove the money back into the envelope and put inside a certain book on the top of the bookcase. A note which had accompanied the money went into the fire, and the captain of the school stood there staring at the dying ashes, with complete disregard of what was going on around him.

Jeff Barber was not very interested in this. His pulses were thumping, his mouth had gone dry. He wanted to run away from temtation, but he could not. For Jeff Barber had a secret passion, and it was betting.

He had lost all his pocket-money with a certain bookie down in the village who was not above taking bets from schoolboys, and Barber believed that if he could only raise the money he would be able to win back all his losses at the forthcoming Westbourne Races.

Betting was now part of him. He had even sold his stamp collection to raise some cash for this purpose, but the amount he had received had been disappointing, and now he saw the dazzling chance of really big money flaunted before his eyes.

He heard Tom counting across the room, withdrew into a window recess to one side, and watched the captain of St Ardens stride past him in the direction of the common room.

As he turned the corner Barber darted out and entered the captain's study. It was not locked. Tom never locked it, for he trusted everybody, and had usually nothing of value in the room to worry about.

Barber's eyes roved over the bookcase. It had been a big, black-bound volume which Tom had used as his hiding place for the unwanted money. In an instant it was out of the shelf, and the registered envelope was in the boy's hand.

He glanced at the postmark.

"Huh! A local one! Wonder who sent him that? I'll bet he's been horse racing and has no right to the money."

deftly he removed two of the ten pound notes, put the others back much as he had found them, and restored them to the book. He set this in it's place and hurried from the study.

Without knowing it, Tom Shale's connection with the Grizzlies had bought crime to St Ardens. One of the boys had become a thief. Temtation had been set in the way of someone to weak-willed to resist it.

Jeff Barber felt the money burning a hole in his pocket. He never knew how he got through morning lessons, and it seemed an age until the midday break allowed him to visit the village on some excuse or other.

When he returned the two ten pound notes were no longer in his pocket.

That day Tom Shale had so much to do he had no time to worry about the money he had recieed in the morning. Not until the tea hour did he really consider the matter again, and then he decided that, as he could never find the rightful owners, he had better it in disguised handwritting to the local hospital. It would at least be doing some good in that way.

Dick Seymour had come to see him about a paper chase they were thinking of getting up, and he stayed so long that Tom was unable to write the note he had intended sending to the hospital with the money.

It was very near six o'clock, and quite dark by the time Dirk departed. Tom took a hasty glance at his watch.

"If I hurry I might just catch the post."

He sat down at the table to write, cleared away some books, and tap-tap-tap! Something tapped three times on his window.

He turned with a jerk, staring at the unscreened window. All was dark outside, and there was a faint drizzle falling. He could see nothing to explain the gentle tapping, although he knew there was no tree near enough to explain the noise.

Tap-tap-tap! He went over to investigate, suspecting a jape, lifted the lower sash, and saw something dangling before his eyes. It was a white piece of paper or an envelope, and in a flash he realised it was on the end of a long fishing rod.

The Grizzlies! They had tried various ways of communicating with him, but this was perhaps the most clever. He pulled the note from the end of the thin rod and hastily scanned it.

He recognised the writing as Stiebel's.

"Dear Chief,-Don't try to spend the notes we sent you this morning. We find that the police have a note of the numbers, and are watching for anyone trying to spend the money."

That was that. The rod had vanished, and he guessed that the men who were holding it were on the outside of the quad wall. His lighted window had been fairly easy to recognise.

He closed the window and went inside. It was a good thing he had not posted his letter earlier. So the numbers of those ten pound notes had been taken, and whoever tried to pass them would be noted and perhaps arrested. The Grizzlies had not been as clever as they had believed, although it was good of them to warn him as they had done.

The best thing he could do was to destroy the whole lot. The fire was burning low, and he kicked a big lump of coal to make it flare. Then he took down the big book from the shelf, locked his door, and took out the notes.

"Five-ten-fifteen-sixteen-seventeen-eighteen."

His eyes bulged. There was only eighteen notes there, and there had been twenty in the morning. He had counted them twice to make certain.

Dumbly he stared at the wad of crisp paper. Where had the other two gone?

Someone had been into his study and taken them. It was a horrible idea, but it was the only one that suited the case. He had been robbed.

He was still staring at the notes when the handle of his door rattled, and the cheery voice of Dick Seymour announced that he had forgotten to mention something.

Hurriedly the captain of the school shoved the notes into his pocket and let his grinning pal in.

"Planning a murder or something, behind locked doors?" asked Dick, looking round him suspiciously, then spotting the big book on the table. It happened to be a copy of Shakespeare. "Well I'm blowed! So you've got a secret vice—reading Shakespeare in your spare time?"

Tom grinned sheepishly, conscious of the notes in his pocket, and then they discussed the forgotten matter for a couple of minutes before Dick Seymour hurried off again.

But Tom Shale's mind had not been on the conversation. The son of Scarface had decided one thing. He must see the Grizzlies at once, and ask there advice about these stolen notes. He must know just what risks he and the unknown thief were running.

PART THREE.

GANG MEETS GANG.

The rian streamed down the windows, and in the dormitories of St Ardens the boys snuggled down under their bedclothes. There were not many of them who could have cared to have been out that night, and certainly none of them would have believed that their captain was at that moment climbing down a couple of knotted sheets from his window.

Tom Shale was going to consult the Grizzlies. He had put on a bathing suit under his oldest raincoat in order not to get his clothes wet, and a few seconds later he dropped into the quad, and looked cautiously around him.

It was a rotten night for going out, and the last on which anyone would expect a boy from the schoolto break bounds. Even old Todd, the gatekeeper, would not be sleeping with one eye open, as he was popularly supposed to do.

In any case, Tom went over the boundary wall into the road beyond. He wasnot risking the gate. Todd had a bulldog that not only slept with one eye, but two ears as well.

He knew where he was going, and it was some way across country. A big country house had been empty and up for let for some time. The Grizzlies had taken possession of it on their own, and behind drawn shutters they had made themselves very comfortable in their secret headquarters. They had told hom to cummunicate with them there if they had ever needed them.

Tom Shale had not expected to do so, but here he was scrambling through the hedges and over ditches in his haste to reach the meeting-place."

By the time the house came in sight it was after midnight, and he was soaked to the skin. The place was in darkness, but whether that was because they were all in bed, or because they had the shutters drawn, he could not tell. He climbed over another wall and entered the grounds.

"Just my luck if there's nobody here tonight!" he muttered, "They might be off on another stunt, but as that message was delivered this evening maybe there's someone here."

He crept through the dripping shrubbery, and wondered whether he ought to knock at the front door or at one of the side doors. Living as they did in constant fear of the police, he did not want to alarm the Grizzlies unnecessarily.

They might shoot him if he did.

He had decided to throw stones at the upper windows, and was stooping in the dark to get some gravel from the path when someone whistled close beside him.

Instantly he flattened himself to the ground and watched. Two dark figures came out from under the lee of the wall, and were joined with two others from the right. A fifth came out from the bushes where climbing roses had been trained over an arch. A sixth could be heard approaching down the drive.

They were so quiet in their movements that for a moment his heartthumped. They were not the Grizzlies. They must be the police! It looked ass though he had arrived in time to see the round-up of his late father's gang.

But something unfamiliar in their outline made him crawl closer and have another look. They were not a bit like police, in fact there was one very fat man with narrow eyes and a loose mouth whom he at once recognised.

"Crawford! It's the Crawford Gang."

He had already learned that his late father's gang had a rival in the shape of a gang of crooks led by a man named Crawford. Already he had seen a scrap between the two gangs. Here was Crawford and his men about to raid the Grizzlies as they slept.

Only one thing was meant. They were going to rob the Grizzlies of anything they had on them in the way of recent loot, and to kill any who resisted. There would be murder in that lonely house before morning if the two gangs met.

The watching boy found himself in a queer position. He had no more wanted to lead the Grizzlies than he did the German Army, but after all he had inherited the gang, and his loyalty was claimed by that, and not by any other gang.

He felt himself growing hot with rage. One of the Crawford crowd was actually forcing one of the lower windows. It would not be long before the crowd slipped inside.

Tom did some quick figuring. These men would be armed, and although the Grizzlies had sent their leader a revolver he had never carried it.

Instead he picked up a large-sized stone and hurled it with all his might at one of the upper-floor windows.

Crash!

There was a tinkle of breaking glass, and a chorus of surptised grunts from the Crawford men.

"Who did that? What was that?"

The man at the window hastily withdrew. On the first floor a window was opened, and a head was poked out.

"Who in heck's that?"

Tom dared not reply, but he had another stone ready, and his aim was accurate. He landed it within an inch of the speaker's ear, and heard him give a grunt of alarm. Another window opened, the Grizzlies were awake.

As for the Crawford gang, they were startled out of their skins by this unwelcome arousing of their foes. They had no idea where the stones had come from, and the six of them withdrew deep into the thickets of laurels to figure things out.

The Grizzlies were coming downstairs. Someone could be heard taking the chain off the front door. Tom braced himself, and as the door was cautiously opened he burst into the open.

"It's the chief, don't shoot!"

Four men with drawn guns received him and after a moments hesitation they stepped aside.

"Come in chief. Never guessed it was you. Why in heck did you have to burst the window to attract our attention? A knock on the door would have done the trick."

"S-sh!" hissed Tom Shale, "The Crawford Gang are here. There's six or seven of them over in those bushes."

He brushed past the startled four, and closed the door after them. He found Nick Stiebel right beside him, and the man's face was twisted more hideously than ever.

"What's this about the Crawford bunch?"

"They're out there in force, with Crawford himself in the lead. How many men have you got here?"

"Only the four of us. The rest are on a job in London, and won't be backuntil tomorrow morning. Do you mean to say—."

Crack!

There came a flash from the letter-box of the door they had just closed, and the man beside Tom spun round twice before crashing to the floor.

"My shoulder! They've got me through the shoulder."

Crack! Crack! Crack!

One of the Crawford men must have dashed up to the door directly it was closed. Now he was emptying his revolver through the letter-box, and it was a marvel none of the others were hit.

They went down flat on the floor until the fusillade had finished, then hurriedly got into a side room. Nick Stiebel was almost livid with rage.

"The skunks! They know there's only a few of us here, and they reckon they've got us. They'd have had us sure enough if you hadn't blown along ,chief. How did you get wise to them?"

"I didn't, confessed the son of Scarface, "I was coming to ask you about those notes. Two of them hve been stolen from me."

Nick Stiebel laughed harshly.

"Then someone's going to get it in the neck. We've got the word that the police had all the numbers, and whoever tries to pass them is to be arrested. The one who robbed you will sure feel sorry for it before long. I advise you to burn the rest, and —."

Crack! Crack!

There was an exchange of shots from the region of the back door. One of the remaining three Grizzlies who was fit to fight had found someone trying to force the door, and had fired through the woodwork. Judging by the howl he had scored a hit.

The wounded gunman had been lifted on to a settee, and Tom Shale found himself holding his gun.

It seemed crazy that he, the captain of the school, should be mixed up in a gang gun-fight of the kind he sometimes seen on the films.

Now that he was there the Grizzlies seem to take it for granted that he would fight at their side.

Crack! Crack!

Somewhere a window was broken,and there was a general rush to that room.

Crawford must have known that the odds were in his favour. He had seperated his men, and was attacking both front and back of the house at once. The house was so lonely that nobody would here the shooting. It was an ideal for rival gangs to settle their long-standing arguments.

Tom gulped as he felt the trigger under his finger. The excitement was gripping him, and in another moment he would forget all about St Ardens and be pumping out lead with the best of them.

He saw a vague shadow at one of the back windows, raised the revolver and fired.

The kick of the gun sent his arm up, he heard a howl of pain, and Nick Stiebel grunted as he brushed past—.

"Good for you, chief. You've winged someone. You're as good a shot as your father."

The son of Scarface Shale flushed.

It looked as though he was taking his father's place without meaning to do so. That shot had been more lucky than skilful, although nobody would ever know.

St Ardens seemed very far away just then.

CHAPTER FIVE.

PART ONE.

TOM'S PEPPER POT.

In a lonely English country house on a moor, miles away from the police, a gang of crooks were waiting with drawn guns.

Outside, a rival gang, under the leadership of a man called Crawford, were hammering at the front and back doors. It was the back door that looked as if it were going to cave in.

the Crawford gang had meant to spring a surprise attack on the Grizzlies, the gang in the house. But this had been prevented by their schoolboy leader butting in. he had just come to the house in time to find the Crawford gang about to enter the house and had raised the alarm inside.

And now Tom Shale, captain of St Ardens, was handling a gun with the rest of the gang and awaiting the fall of the door.

Tom Shale hardly knew whether he was frightened or whether he was enjoying himself. He discovered he had fired all the shots from his revolver, and he had hit at least one man. For a captain of St Ardens school this was a strange manner to be spending the night, but Tom Shale was not out of bounds at two o'clock in the morning through any choice of his own.

Tom had been the popular captain of his school with no care in all the world, before his father had died. Captain Thomas Shale had died in Paris, and not until later did the boy learn the truth of the affair.

He was then informed that his father had been the leader of a gang of crooks known as the Grizzlies, and that he had been shot in a fray with the French police whilst leading his gang to rob a jeweller's shop.

Proof of this was not the only thing that came to Tom. The Grizzlies came to England and hunted him up. There was some kind of inter-gang quarrel going on about who should be the leader after Scarface Shale, and rather than split up over the matter they had decided that the son of Scarface should take over the leadership.

Tom had protested that it was crazy to expect him, a schoolboy, to be mixed up with a gang of scoundrels, but they hadtold him he must either agree or he would be killed and his father's reputation blackened in the eyes of everyone.

Whereupon Tom had squared his shoulders and made a private oath that if he led them it would be for his own ends.

So far he had managed to spoil every raid they had since undertaken, but tonight he found himself in a rather different position.

It was a question of his late father's gang against the Crawford bunch, and from what he had seen of Crawford and his men he hated them even more than he did the men he was forced to mix with.

So he was fighting at their side in this lonely house, wondering if he would escape with his life, and if he did so how would he get back to St Ardens before roll-call in the morning.

Crash! Crash!

The door was certainly giving, and when it gave he saw all hopes of escaping further bloodshed vanishing.

Then he remembered the memorable occasion on which the St Ardens boys had withstood the assault of twice their number of "townies" in the football field pavilion last autumn, and how they had prevented the door from being battered down.

He ducked through a door into the big kitchen, rummaged about and discovered what he wanted.

A tin in his hand, he raced up the stairs to the first floor, hearing Crawford urging his men to renew their efforts. One half of the door was collapsing inwards. The entire Crawford bunch was tightly packed outside.

Tom made for a window directly over that door, opened it quietly, leaned out, and took the top of the tin he had snatched from the kitchen.

He emptied the contents boldly downwards, and the next moment it sounded as though half-a-dozen minor explosions had occurred.

They were not explosions, but sneezes. The men at the door dropped their battering-ram to seize their hankerchiefs. Sneeze after sneeze rang out, and he could hear them moaning and gasping at the smarting of their eyes.

He grinned to himself as he hurled the tin far from him.

"Nothing like an ounce or two of pepper for breaking up a crowd!"

Down below Nick Stiebel and the other Grizzlies had realised that something extraordinary was delaying the assault on the door. They crept up and emptied half-a-dozen shots through the broken door, and that completed the defeat of the Crawford men. Sneezing and blinded by pepper, they fled for the cover of the woods, and Tom joined the others in the hall.

He was still chuckling.

The three Grizzlies looked at him in admiration as they attempted to stem the flow of blood from the wound of their comrade.

"You sure have got your head screwed on the right way, chief," drawled Stiebel, "I'd never have thought of that."

"How long do you think this bunch will hang around?" asked the captain of St Ardens eagerly, "I've got to get back before roll-call, or there'll be dickens to pay."

"Aw, forget it! If they make any trouble for you at the school we'll come and fill those masters of yours full of lead," was Nick Stiebel's rather alarming offer, "What was that you were saying about those notes we sent you this morning?"

"Two of the ten pound notes have been stolen. Someone at the school must have pinched them. Now you say the numbers are known to the police. Is that certain?"

"Absolutely certain. Whoever tries to cash those notes is for it. You ought to have been more carefull with the dough, chief."

Tom Shale flushed.

He had not asked the gang to send him two hundred pounds as his share of some unlawful deal they had carried out without his knowledge. He had not even known what to do with the money, and had hidden it in a book in his study. That evening he had discovered that two of the notes had vanished.

Someone at St Ardens was a thief!

"I've got to try and find out who did it and make them hand the notes over," he mused, half aloud, "When do you think this Crawford crowd will go away?"

"Any time before dawn. They expected to take us by surprise, and now they realise we're wide awake. They've got at least two injured. I guess they'll beat it quite soon, in case Slim Dolman and the rest of the boys return."

Tom sighed.

It all seemed so hopelessly unreal to him. Only a few weeks ago, he had been interested in nothing except his work and the football teams. Now he was plunged into crime, and every day it became worse and worse. Already he had been caught by the Headmaster sneaking out at night to meet the Grizzlies. He had nearly been expelled on that occasion. The next time it would be a cert.

"I've got to slip through as soon as possible," he said, "I daren't risk stoping much longer. I'll burn the rest of the notes, and the missing two I'll try and trace. A bright lot of good you fellows have been to me since I took over my father's job!"

they looked duly ashamed of themselves. It did not enter their heads that their continual failures lately had been entirely due to their new leader's clever efforts. Since Tom had taken over the leadership they had not gained a single profit out of any of their deals.

Half an hour later they heard the Crawford bunch pile into a waiting car and drive away.

It was safe for Tom to turn out into the wet night again. He was glad he wore only his old bathing costume under his oldest raincoat. There was no chance of wet clothing giving him away in the morning

PART TWO.

SUSPENSE AND ARREST.

Tom Shale had returned safely, and was in the breakfast hall with the rest at the usual time in the morning, rather sleepy-eyed because of his lost rest, but actually wide awake.

From his position at the top of the senior's table he scanned the area of faces around him. Who out of those several hundred boys could have been responsible for stealing the twenty pounds. It seemed a crazy thing to ask. There were some mischievious young rascals in the school, and some imps whose ability to make trouble was extraordinary, but a thieve was another matter. He could have sworn that there was nobody amonst the seniors with the makings of a thief in them. Probably he himself was the only one out of the whole lot who had ever come in touch with thieves.

Yet the money had vanished, and it was hard to know who could have entered his study. Someone must have seen him put it there, and had taken advantage of his absence to collect the twenty pounds. It was a vast sum of money for a schoolboy. What could have any fellow done with it?

The trouble was that Tom could not complain to the masters and have a search made. If he did that he would have to explain how he came in possession of so much money, and then the fat would be in the fire. He must depend upon himself entirely.

All through the morning lessons he brooded over the matter, and his work suffered in consequence. Twice he was ticked off for inattention, and he was heartily glad when the noon bell rang.

Back to his study he went to try and puzzle out any fresh clues, but Tom had not the makings of a deyective in him. He trusted everyone too much for that, and for the life of him he could not think of anyone who had been near his study at the time he had opened the registered letter which had contained the money.

His paks, Dick Seymour and Reddy Trotter tried to get him to come out for a walk, but he made some excuse to remain where he was, and he only left his study when he went down to the dinning-room for lunch.

The hubbub, and the sight of all those jolly faces, made him forget his worries. He got tangled in an argument with Stoke of the Upper Fifth, and was still hot in the midst of this when there was a sudden silence in the hall.

He looked up in some surprise, then he went cold all over.

The Headmaster, Dr Lumley, had just entered, and with him were two uniformed policemen and a plain-clothes man who was obviously a detective.

The Doctor held up his hand, which explained the silence, and now he was mounting the platform at the end of the room. The plain-clothes man followed him, while the uniformed policemen remained close to the door.

"Iask silence," boomed the Doctor, "Something very serious indeed has occurred. It is very painful to me to have to speak about it."

Tom Shale was clutching at the edge of the table. The police! He could already feel the cold chill of the handcuffs on his wrists.

He felt sure they had come for him. Something had happened to the gang. Someone had given away his connection with the Grizzlies, and there was to be a public arrest.

He looked round as though he thought of bolting, but there was not the slightest chance of that.

The Doctor was speaking.

"A certain boy in this hall has recently has been dealing with a beting agent in the village. He has been placing bets with this man on vasious races, and yesterday he placed a big bet of no less than twenty pounds. Unfotunately for the boy the notes he gave the bookmaker were stolen, and the numbers known to the police. That is why I am forced to suffer the indignity of seeing the police in my dining hall."

The Doctor's voice broke. It must have the bitterest moment of his life.

From somewhere at one side of the hall came a gasp of alarm, then the Headmaster hardened his voice and growled.

"Stand up, Geoffrey Barber!"

Jeff Barber! Who would have thought it?

Tom Shale nearly gave himself away by jumping to his feet. Jeff Barber! Why had he not thought of that before? Barber was a Fifth Form boy who had a reputation of being a sneak, and there had been whispers amonst the juniors that he backed horses.

Barber was now on his feet, and the uniform policemen had stepped forward and taken him by the arm.

"I didn't know they were stolen! I didn't steal them!" screamed the lad, "He must have stolen them before he hid them in that book. I tell you—."

The police hustled him out through the side door, and the Headmaster mopped his face.

"Get on with your lunch!" he ordered, and hurried out after what must have been one of the hardest tasks of his life.

Uproar broke out.

Everyone was talking at once.

Everyone asked his neighbour what it all meant, and where Barber could have got the notes. At least half a dozen asked Tom Shale, but his mind was too far away even for him to hear what they were saying.

His head was buzzing.

He found himself swallowing food without knowing what it was he ate. At any moment now that door might open and someone would come in and call his name.

Barber would be sure to say where he had got the notes, and then Tom would be summoned to explain how they come to be in that book on his book-shelf. His father's secret was on the verge of being discovered.

But somehow the meal finished, and nobody came to call him. The boys crowded out into the corridors and into the quad, but there was nothing for them to see. The car with the police and the prisoner had been whisked away. It was said that the Head had gone with them.

Then all to soon the bell for afternoon classes summoned them to the usual grind, and Tom Shale was not the only one who was innatentive. Every time the door opened he thought someone was coming for him. He was the most surprised person in the school when the afternoon finished and nobody had challenged him.

Then as he made his way to his study with Dick Seymour, the expected summons came. One of the masters told him that the Headmaster wanted him in his study.

Tom drew a deep breath and squared his shoulders. So the moment had come at last. He must face it like a man, and make a clean breast of everything.

When he entered the Head's study, Dr Lumley was resting his face on his two hands. He looked ten years older when he raised his head. The disgrace had weighed heavily on him.

"Sit down, Shale! I want to ask your advice."

Tom sat.

It was lucky he did so, for his knees were about to give way. This was hardly the greeting he had expected.

"It's about that wretched boy,Barber," went on the Head, "He has got himself in an awful mess. The police do not for a moment believe he actually stole the money from the originl owners, who seem to have been Amsterdam diamond merchants, but they are inclined to think that he found the notes and gave way to temptation. The trouble is that the wretched lad won't open his mouth. He will not say where he found or obtained the twenty pounds. I wonder if you can throw any light on the subject?"

"I, sir?" asked Tom, his mouth drying.

"Yes, I wondered if you had heard any talk about where Barber had been lately, or whether he had received a registered letter or a message from any outsider. Sometimes rumours go round amonst the boys and you have more chance than most of us of hearing them. Anything you might have heard will be of help to us."

Tom breathed again. So thanks to the stubborness of Barber his secret was still safe.

He pretended to think.

"I'm sorry, sir, but I've heard nothing much about Barber for a long time. He isn't a popular boy, and I did once hear some fags saying something about him backing horses. They had found the slips in the ashes of his fire. But I know nothing that would help, sir."

"Thank you, Shale, I was afraid you would not. Maybe after a night in the cells the wretched lad will think better of it and give an explanation."

With a nod he dismissed the captain of the school, and outside the door Tom Shale mopped his face.

He did not want to go through an other interview like that.

PART THREE.

THE GANG TAKE A HAND.

In spite of the efforts of the authorities and the school to keep things quiet. It became known around the neighbourhood that one of the boys was at the local lockup charged with being in possession of banknotes known to have been stolen abroad. The romour spread and grew alarmingly. In the village it was said that Dr Lumley himself had been arrested.

Twenty-four hours had passed, and still Barber refused to explain anything. What he expected to gain by keeis mouth shut nobody could explain, but he refused to utter a word of explanation.

Those twenty-four hours for Tom were terrible ones. He looked and felt quite ill. Even his pals kidded him about it. It was the suspence that told. He was expecting the bust-up to come every moment. And the trouble was he felt so helpless. He did not see what he could do to save himself.

He hadcthought of the Grizzlies, but what could they do?they might suggest that he should bolt from the school, but that would mean definitely throwing in his lot with them and becoming a professional crook. He had no idea of doing that.sooner than that he would make a clean confession of the whole thing.

It was after school the following afternoon, and Dick and he were cycling towards the village to make purchases at one of the shops when round the corner came a car driven at more than sixty miles an hour.

It missed them only by inches, nearly ran up the opposite bank, got on to the crown of the road again, and procceeded on it's way again at even greater speed.

"Silly asses!" roared Dick, almost falling from his machine, "They might have killed us. I hope the cops get them for speeding, and I'll jolly well give evidence against them if I have the chance."

his voice rose excitedly, but Tom did bot hear it. Tom Shale was gazing after the cloud of dust thrown up by the car. He had rcognised the car as the one owned by the Grizzlies. Why the terrific hurry?

Everything was explained a few moments later when they entered the main street of the little town and found everything in disorder and confusion.

People were crowded into shop-doors or in groups at the street corners. A score or more were outside the police station where two or three were picking up a uniformed figure from the pavement.

A car had turned over broadside on across the front of a fruit shop, and somewhere inside the police station a whistle was shrilling.

Everyone seemed to be talking at once.

"What's the matter? What's the row?" demanded the boys.

"Matter enough! This country is becoming more like America every day!" snorted someone, "A car drove up to the door of the police station as cool as you like, and three men got out and rushed inside. We heard shots, saw Constable Short comes reeling down the steps and falls in a heap, then the three men appear carrying a boy."

"A boy?"

"Yes, the kid they've had from your school this last twenty-four hours. They were half-pushing and half-carrying him. They bundled him into the car, fired a few shots over our heads, scared Bill Jones into driving into a window,and then lit out at sixty miles an hour. They say that Constable Short is badly hurt."

"Gosh!" Dick's eyes were sparkling, "What cheek! Just like you see on the films, Tom. These modern gangsters have got some nerve. What in the name of wonder would they want with Jeff Barber"

Tom was not replying. He was forcing his way the crowd to try and find out if it was true that Jeff Barber had been kidnapped from the police station.

It was true enough, and Constable Short had been badly wounded in trying to stop the gangsters from entering. They had all worn hankerchiefs tied over their faces and it had been impossible to recognise any of them.

That did not matter to Tom. He knew who they were right enough. The Grizzlies had done this, and he could not imagine why. They must have heard from local gossip what had happened to Barber, but why in the name of wonder had they gone to all this risk and trouble?

One thing was certain. He must get in touch with the gang as soon as possible and find out their game. He must put a stop to it. What was the use of being their leader if he could not do that.

But Dick Seymour would not leave him. He stuck closer than a brother. He could not be shaken off, and Tom was scared to make too thin an excuse to get rid of him. It would have looked suspicious.

Then on their way back to the school Tom had a punture, and they were obliged to push their machines the rest of the way, it was getting near roll-call when they arrived. There was no time for him to go out again.

Roll-call was over, and they were surrounded by an excited crowd of boys who had heard something of what had occurred in the village and who knew Dick and Tom had been down there. They were asking a thousand questions.

Dick was only too pleased to answer, but Tom was short and impatient. Something must be done about Barber. For all he knew—.

"Tom Shale! Hi Shale, there's a man at the gate with a message for you," shouted someone, "Old Todd asked me to tell you. A chap's found something of your's he says."

Tom scowled.

To the best of his knowledge he had not lost anything, but themessage was definate enough, and he hurried across the quad leaving Dick talking to the crowd.

Todd waved him to the partly opened gate where a dim figure stood. With a start Tom recognised it as Oakley, one of the less important members of the gang.

The man looked shabby and at once began to whine.

"Your one of the gents who was cycling back from the village this afternoon?"

"Yes, but—."

"Then you dropped your saddle-bag. I picked it up, and here it is. If it's worth a tanner to you, sir, I'll be obliged. I had to walk a mile to get here."

Tom took the new brown saddle-bag, and blinked. He was just about to say it was not his, and he had never seen it before, when the man winked.

He quickly collected his wits.

"That's fine! Thanks very much. I'm very pleased to get it back. Here's a tanner for you. Very much obliged."

The gangster touched his hat and withdrew. Todd closed and locked the gate, told Tom he was lucky to get the bag again, and went back into his lodge.

Tom could hardly wait until he reached the next corner to open the bag. Of course there was a message inside. The gangsters must have recognised him when they nearly ran him over with Dick Seymour, and they had chosen this clever method of communicating with him.

There was a slip of paper wrapped in a greasy rag. He flattened it out.

"Dear Chief," it said, "Don't worry any more about that kid talking about the notes he pinched from you. We've seen to that. He won't talk."

That was all, but it left Tom going hot and cold by turns. No more need for him to worry! What did that mean? What had they done to Jeff Barber? Knowing how utterly callous they were he knew it was quite possible tha they had killed Barber to silence him.

CHAPTER SIX.

PART ONE.

THE EMPTY HOUSE.

Tom Shale wanted to get out of St Ardens School tonight in order to see the members of the gang of crooks called "The Grizzlies." But it was far too dangerous because policemen were swarming all over the countryside. As a matter of fact, fifth extra men had been brought in to help the locals.

It was not often that the peaceful countryside around St Ardens School was so disturbed. Never in the history of the town had such a thing happened. Armed gangsters had raided the police station, had shot down one of the constables, and made off with a prisoner from the police cells.

That prisoner was one of St Ardens boys, and Tom Shale, the captain of the school had more reason to be interested in him than anybody, for the younster who had been kidnapped or rescued by the gangsters knew something about Tom which wound have brought his present mode of life to an end.

Tom Shale, quite unwillingly, was leading a double life. At St Ardens he was the respected captain, liked by the boys and the masters, and well deserving of their trust. Outside the school he was the leader of a gang of desperate crooks.

It was a strange situation for an English schoolboy, and it had only come about since the death of his father.

Captain Shale had always been making mysterious business trips to France and other countries, but not until his deathdid his son learn the terrible truth that his father was no other than Scarface Shale, the leader of a gang known as the "Grizzlies."

Scarface Shalehad been liked by his men, and under his leadership they had been one of the most successful gangs in the world. When he had died there had been some quarrel as to his successor to their leader and rather than split up the gang they had decided that his son, Tom, should follow him.

Tom had been summonedand aquaintedwith the facts, and had been told that if he refused he would be killed and his father's name publicly disgraced.

Finally he had pretended to agree, but in his heart he had sworn that they would make no profit out of his leadership. He would lead them for his own ends, and spoil all their raids.

So far, he had succeeded in carrying out this double life, but when the gang had sent him two hundred pounds as his share of some crooked deal they had carried out abroad without his knowledge, he had hidden the unwanted money in a book in his study. Unfortunately he had been seen by a rather weak-willed Fifth Former named Jeff Barber, and Barber had been backing horses and had lost heavily.

The Fifth Former had stolen twenty pounds of the money and had backed a horse with a village bookmaker, but the numbers of the missing notes had been known to the police, and Barber was arrested.

It was because they feared that Barber might tell the police where he had got those notes that the Grizzlies had raided the police station and carried him off.

They sent word to Tom telling him not to worry.

Not to worry?   That was all very well. He knew very well that they were likely to murder Jeff Barber to silence him. If that happened he would feel responsible, yet what could he do? He could not get out to communicate with them, as their headquarters was in a country house several miles across country and he had no means of getting there.

Roll-call had gone, and the boys were preparing to go their dormitories when there was fresh excitement.

Police had arrived at St Ardens to ask if the missing boy had by any chance returned to the school.

Of course the Doctor had to tell them that he had seen nothing of Barber, and Tom Shale wondered whether he ought not to go and make a clean breast of thing to the police superintendent who was just leaving the Doctor's quarters.

If it had been a case of merely getting himself into trouble he would not have hesitated, but his father's name would be dragged through the mud if he gave away the Grizzlies. They had promised him that.

He was still standing there undecided when Dr Lumley called him over.

"Shale, the superintendent has decide that he would like one of the senior boys to be with the police tonight in case they get in touch with Barber. He thinks the boy has been rescuedagainst his will, and if they can get in touch with him he wants one of you to play a part of a third party. There is a certain amount of sense in what he says, but of course I do not want to expose any of you to risk. If you would care to go with him—."

"I would, sir!" Tom surprised himself by his own eagerness. He saw that there might be a chance of getting in touch with the Grizzlies. It solved his problem of how to get out of school. "I certainly would like to help the superintendent."

Superintendent Giles was a typical country police officer, but quite efficient. As he presently drove Tom away in his car he told him what he had done to trace the raiders.

He had phoned all the surrounding counties to close the roads and stop every car that passed. They had not got the number of the car, but they had a general idea of it's type, and they had circulated the description.

"Ido not think it has got very far away. It is my idea that they have carried Barber to some hiding place within a few miles. Nothing has been heard of them passing through Balcombe, and if they'd gone on the road they left by they would have gone through that village. Maybe they are sheltering in some woods, or in a lonely house."

Tom's pulses thumped.

The superintendent was very near the truth when he guessed a lonely house. The house in which the gang had their headquarters was one supposedly empty with notices of sale plastered all over it.

The next two hours passed for him like a nightmare. The superintendant visited his various posts around the district and got their reports. So far they had no trace of the gang or it's prisoner. Tom did not voice his fear that the Grizzlies might have did away with Jeff and scattered. Every moment he expected to hear the dreaded news that Barber's body had been found.

The night drew on, yet Tom did not feel at all sleepy. There was far too much excitement. With the superintendent he went everywhere, and it must have been four o'clock in the morning when the at last startling news came through.

The local police had received information that men had been seen entering a lonely house not a mile away. One of the constables had reported seeing fresh wheelmarks on the drive, and there was no doubt that cars had been in and out of there frequently, in spite of the fact that everyone believed it to have been empty for months.

The superintendent was very excited, and at once set off towards the spot with two constables and Tom Shale. The police were in high spirits, but Tom was trying to quieten his pounding heart, for he knew that the place they were gto visit was the house where the gang had their headquarters.

The game was up.

In twenty minutes or so they would give him away if they saw him with the police.

They would think he was a traitor.

He tried to make some excuse to leave the superintendent's car, but Giles would not let him.

"No my lad, if your friend Barber is a prisoner in that house, he'll be mighty glad to see a familiar face there amongst his rescuers. You stick close to us, and you'll see some fun. Half my men are armed, and if there's trouble it won't all on one side."

Tom groaned inwardly.

There was nothing he could do about it. He had to see it through.

The police cars pulled up a quarter of a mile from the house which he had already twice visited . Constables came out from the hedges and reported that nobody had left the place during the last half hour. The police were closing in. the superintendent meant to rush the place from front and back.

Tom hoped his face did not look too white. Not knowingwhat the boy was suffering the police would probably think he was nervous.

PART TWO.

GANGSTERS AT ST ARDENS.

The superintendent had given the signal. Men advanced from all sides upon the silent house. It was in darkness, but that might mean nothing. Twenty policemen very soon were going to penetrate it's secrets.

They reached the front door and the back door at the same time, and their surprise at finding already bearing the sign of a battering was not shared by Tom Shale. He had been present when a few nights earlier a rival gang had tried to enter the Grizzlies headquarters.

Because of the shattered door the police were able to enter the place without too much trouble, and Tom winced at the expectation of the shooting that was to come. He knew that Nick Stiebel, Slim Dolman, and the rest of them, would not give in withouut a struggle.

But minutes succeeded minutes, and there wasno shooting. The police over-ran the house, and Tom could hardly stand the suspence. Then came the news that although traces of recent occupation had been found, there was not a man in the place.

Tom's sigh of relief would have been heard if the police had not groaned their disappointment aloud.

The superintendent was particuarly angry.

"Too late! This means that they had warning of our coming and changed their roosting-place. Now we have to start the hunt all over again."

Just before dawn came fresh news. A car answering the description of the wanted one had been found abandoned some miles from the village. There was no clue to the identity of the missing occupants.

Although he was still desperately anxious about Barber, Tom could not help chuckling to himself at the cleverness of the Grizzlies. How had they done it? How had they slipped the police search and got clean away? What had they done with their prisoner?

Daylight came, and new relays of men took up the search. Tom was advised to go back to the school and as there seemed no chance for him to meet any of the Grizzlies, he obeyed.

His breakfast was a tremendous one. Dr Lumley questioned him about the night's happenings, and looked as though he had not slept a wink of sleep himself. He suggested that Tom had better take the morning off and get some sleep.

The captain of St Ardens was glad to get between the sheets after a quick tub. And he was hardly settled down with his head on the pillow when his feet touched something that rustled.

Paper! Who had put paper in his bed? Visions of a jape prepared during his absence, with some kind of surprise due to burst upon him at any moment, made him hurriedly kick the bedclothes aside.

But there was nothing more alarmingthan a large sheet of white paper folded on four,and when he sat up and opened this out he found himself staring at the following message.

"Dear Chief,—Six of us and the kid are in the old furnace-room below the school. We guessed this would be the only safe spot in the district. We are relying on you to bring us grub to last us through the day. We'll clear out when night comes again."

Tom Shale nearly bounded from his bed in alarm. The Grizzlies here in St Ardens! Things were getting crazier and crazier, madder and madder, every moment.

Thinking they could rely on the son of Scarface Shale, the gangsters who had carried out the raid on the police station had sought refuge in the school itself. One of them had actually crept up to find their chief during the night, and discovering that he was absent had placed this note where his bare feet would not fail to find it.

Tom knew the furnace room they mentioned well. When coal had been used for the school central-heating, the furnace down there, had always been in use, but since oil-heating had been introduced only half the space was necessary, and the second cellar was empty but for a certain amount of old lumber.

Six desperate men and Jeff Barber were lurking down there! His head reeled at the thought.

The risk they were taking was tremendous, and in any case how did they expect him to take them food? Six men not to mention Jeff Barber could eat like a horse. He would need a full-sized hamper.

He lay there for a time thinking it out. He dared not turn over and go to sleep and try to forget them, for he knew the Grizzlies well enough to realise they would get desperate and come out on the prowl for food themselves. If they met anyone who tried to stop them there might be more shooting. He must do anything to prevent that, and in any case he wanted to discover what had happened to Barber.

He rose and dressed.

If he saw the Doctor he could make the excuse that he was over-tired and restless.

As the school was at lessons the place was almost deserted. It was a long time Tom had crept down the corridor leading to the school store-room and pantry. As Third and Fourth Form boys he and some others had sometimes raided the stores, but he had never expectedto be doing this again, and in broad daylight.

Mrs Gregory, the housekeeper, had portioned out her stores for the day, and was doubtless in the kitchen weighing and measuring out each boys portion. Knowing the boys were under the eyes of their masters, she had not troubled to remove her keys from the lock of the store-room, and Tom Shale let himself in.

he looked round at the laden shelves and felt his pulses beating faster than they had ever done when he was younger. But a great deal more depended upon this raid than those when he was in the Forth. Then at the most being caught meant a liking and being gated for the rest of the term, but for the captain of the school to be caught under such circumstances could only mean discovery of his whole secret.

What could he take to satisfy the gangsters? There was bacon and sack of sugar and flour. They were useless. He saw big tins of dry biscuits and grabbed one of these. A bigcheese was tucked insidehis jacket, and he stuffed his pocket with raisins.

He crept out again and relocked the door. The chances were that Mrs Gregory would not discover what had happened until her next stocktaking day.

He took the cellar steps to the furnace room, guessing that the janitor would be having his usual eleven o'clock smoke at that time. He slipped round behind the coal bunkers, and into the dark passage leading to the old furnace room.

He had not gone many paces when two strong handsshot out from nowhere and closed around his throat. Something cold and hard was pressed against the side of his neck.

"One word out of you and your a dead one!"

He recognised the voice of Nick Stiebel, but could not utter a word in reply, the pressure on his windpipe was too strong.

The unseen hands dragged him forward, he felt a blanket brush his face, and then found himself in a dimly lit vault where two candle ends burnt on upturned bricks. The blanket was over the door and had shut in the light.

A grunt came from Stiebel.

"Gosh, if it isn't the Chief!"

His hands relaxed at once, and Tom cleared his throat painfully.

"You big chump! Trying to make me drop this food and spoil it? Why didn't you look who you were jumping on?"

Stiebel looked very sheepish, and from the dark corners where they had been sprawling on old sacking the five or six other members of the gang rose and crowded round him.

"Chief! Got something to eat?"

He pushed the buscuits and cheese upon them, unoaded the raisins, and looked anxiously about him.

"Where's Barber?" he asked, trying hard not to show the fear in his voice.

One of them grinned and pointed his thumb in the direction of the old boiler in the far corner.

"He's tied up and shoved in there out of the way. We didn't hurt him more than we could help. We just frightened him into telling us the truth. He's a poor specimen and it's a good thing he kept his mouth shut as long as he did, Chief, or he'd have busted things up for you."

"Can he hear or see me?" whispered Tom, "I don't want to be recognised!"

"Naw!" grunted Slim Dolman, between mouthfuls of food, "He can't do either, but what we want to know is what can we do with him. We can slip out of here tonight and make our getaway. It'll be easy to find new headquarters if we're not loaded down with him, but we can't tag him along everywhere. Will you give us permission to bump hom off and hide his body in that boiler? He might not be found for years and—."

Tom almost choked with horror.

"No!" he rasped, "If you hurt him I'll make you all sorry for it as sure as I'm the son of Scarface! He's not going to be harmed. What's more, you've all got to get out of here. It was madness to come here."

"Dunno about that, Chief," protested someone, "It's about the safest place we could find. They'll never think of looking here, and if it wasn't that we had other jobs on hand we wouldn't mind hiding here for a few nights. But we want to get out tonight, and it only means settling what to do with the kid. He can't go loose, or he'd spill the beans at once about you."

Tom thought hard, hands clenched, lips tight. He had the fate of a schoolmate in the balance, and although he was not a friend of Jeff Barber, and although he knew the boy was not a credit to the school, he felt that out of loyalty to St Ardens he must treat him lightly.

"He might be kept out of the way for a time only," he murmured, "If there was some way of—."

He broke off quickly.

In the outer cellar he had suddenly heard footsteps, and the voice of Dr Lumley.

"The men would come today when we have trouble enough," he was saying to the janitor, "But you had better take them in and show them, Jacobs."

PART THREE.

BENEATH THE SCHOOL.

Tom Shale swung round on the gangsters.

"Hide yourselves quickly. That's the Headmaster, and he's sending some builders men in here to investigate. There's been damp working up into the common room overhead, and he's asked them to look into things. Quickly!"

More than one of the group dived his hand into a pocket and withdrew a revolver, but Tom Shale had set an example by diving for one of the old bins, which had contained coal in the days when the furnace was used. The candles had been extinguished at once.

It took them no more than twenty seconds to disappear from view, and by that time old Jacobs had finished scraping matches and had a latern lit.

They heard him grumbling as he led the way.

"You would come just when it was my smoke time. If you ask me it's that corner over there by the boiler. The wet fair rises out of the ground there."

Then a grunt came from him as he blundered into the hanging blanket which nobody had had time to remove. It knocked him across the face, and he ripped it away impatiently.

"Drat that thing! How did it get here?"

He shone the lamp around suspiciously, but there was nothing more to be seen. The gangsters were all out of sight, and the big boiler sheltered their prisoner.

The two builders' men went to the corner indicated and knelt down to examine the ground, tapping the brickwork and hunting for the cause of the damp. They did not know that they were within six feet of the boy whom all the country was looking.

Tom scarcely dared breathe. Every moment he expected something to happen to give them away. If it did he knew a volley of shots would follow, for the gangsters would never consent to be trapped in that cellar. He would be unable to hold them in check.

He felt a terrible desire to sneeze, and grasped his nose firmly between finger and thumb in order to check the feeling. To his relief the sneeze did not develop, and the men at the other end made a good deal of noise with their knocking.

Seeing that his advice was not wanted, Jacobs set the latern down by the boiler and retired to the outer cellar to finish his pipe.

The workmen began to prise up some of the bricks. The gangsters stirred uneasily. They were far from comfortable, and it loked as though the builders' men had come to stay.

The slight rustling in the coal bins was heard.

"Rats in these cellars," said one of the workmen.

"Always is," grunted the other, and they left it at that.

Minutes passed, and Tom began to get cramped. He guessed the others were in a similar plight, and he hoped the workmen would hurry up before trouble commenced.

Presently they went, telling the janitor they would return that afternoon with tools.

"That settles it," grunted Nick Stiebel, as he climbed from the bin, "We've got to get out before then. I'm not going to squat in that bin again for anyone. I'd sooner shoot my way out."

The blanket was replaced and the candles re-lit. Tom talked earnestly with them and for once they listened. He was their chosen leader and he knew the school and it's grounds. He suggested that during the janitor's lunch-hour they should sneak out with their prisoner and hide in the summer house of the Doctor's private garden.

At that time of the year it was never used, and there was a loft overhead which could be made into a useful hiding-place.

In the end they agreed to do this, and Dolman said.

"Tonight we'll clear out altogether. It's not fair to you, Chief, for us to stop here. Now about the kid. You want him looked after but kept out of the way for a while. I've got the idea. There's the skipper of a tramp steamer sailing from a port not thirty miles from here who's a pal of mine. I did him a good turn once, and he'll do me one. We'll shanghai the kid aboard the "Saucy Lou" and he'll go to South America and back. The skipper can pretend to think him a stowaway, and make him work his passage. It might make a man out of him. The kids no good to himself or anyone else now."

Tom Shale did not quite like the idea, but it was the best they could agree upon. He knew that if he made it too difficult for the gang they would settle the matter by killing Barber.

"Alright! How long will he be away?"

"About four months. By the time he gets back you'll have decided to quit this school and throw in your lot with us, Chief," said Dolman.

Tom Shale did not think so, but he nodded and left it at that. Four months grace was not bad, and Jeff Barber certainly deserved some punishment for his way of behaving. He had discraced the school.

Arrangments were made for the gang to communicate with him when they found their new headquarters. They insisted upon this, although the captain of St Ardens would rather they had never tried to get in touch with him again.

Jacobs was somewhere outside cleaning out his pipe with a piece of straw. It was easy enough for Tom to slip through and reach the yard. He did not want to pass the store-room again in case he met Mrs Gregory. It might be awkward if she remembered meeting him there after the biscuit tin and cheese was missed.

He dodged along close to the wall so as to be out of range of the windows, and let himself in by the side door which led to the stairs and his own room.

He was halfway up these stairs and was congratulating himself upon having done it very successfully, when he heard the rustle of a silken gown. Dr Lumley came round the corner with a bundle of books under his arm.

Tom stepped aside to let him pass, and hurriedly prepared his excuse for being out of bed, but it was not at his face the Doctor looked. Dr Lumley pointed at his legs, and in a voice quivering with surprise and anger demanded.

"Where on Earth have you been to get your clothes in such a state, Shale? I gave you permission to stop in bed to rest, not to go playing amounst the coal. What have you been doing?"

Coal!

Tom looked down and chilled with horror. He had forgotten those coal-bins were thick with black dust. His clothing from the waist down was as black as the working clothes of a coal miner.

CHAPTER SEVEN.

IN A TIGHT CORNER.

"Coal,sir!" Tom Shale was playing desperately for time, "Coal!"

"Yes, coal!" snorted Dr Lumley, the Headmaster of St Ardens, "Don't pretend you fail to understand what I mean. What have you been doing amonst the coal? What were you in the cellar for?"

the captain of St Ardens had never felt so small in all his life. From the waist down he was black with coal dust, and had not even noticed until he met the Head on the stairs.

"I'd rather not tell you, sir."

He was still playing for time. What could he say? In the furnace house underneath the school at that very moment were half a dozen desperate men, gangsters, wanted all over Europe for various crimes. At any cost he must distract attention from that cellar.

For the gangsters were members of the "Grizzlies" and Tom Shale, the respected captain of St Ardens, was their leader!

It was an amazing situation for any scholboy to be in, but it was not Tom's fault. Until his father had died he had believed him to be some kind of business man with interests which took him frequently to the continent.

Then had come the news of his death in Paris, and the horrible disclosure that he was no other than Scarface Shale, the leader of the Grizzlies, one of the most dreaded gangs of crooks in existence.

Tom had been horrified, but the Grizzlies had told him he must now assume theleadership in succession to his father. If he refused they were not only going to kill him, but to broadcast his father's disgrace.

So Tom had been forced into the leadership of a gang of desperate criminals, although he had sworn privately that he would lead them for his own ends and prevent them pulling off any big raids.

One of his scoolboys, named Jeff Barber, had discovered something of Tom's secret, and the gang had promptly kidnapped him to prevent him telling the police who had arrested him. This Fifth Form boywas now down in the cellar with the gangsters, and they intended stopping there until nightfall, for the district was being combed by the police.

It was a bad enough situation for Tom to be in, and it would be the very worst of luck if it was all given away by some coal dust.

"So you would rather not tell!" growled Dr Lumley. Recent events had upset his temper and his nerves, "Do I understand that you refuse to tell, Shale?"

Tom nodded miserably. He could think of no suitable story the occasion.

Dr Lumley looked hard at him. Like all the other masters he rather admired Tom, and it was a great disappointment to him to find the lad getting into trouble. Then a thought struck him.

"Does it concern someone else? Is that why you won't tell me?"

The boy snatched at the excuse.

"Yes, sir. As a matter of fact it concerns several other people, and it wouldn't be fair for me to say anything. But in any case I've done nothing wrong, sir. I hadn't noticed that I'd slipped in the coal dust."

"Hm!" Anxiously he watched the Doctor's face. His one fear was that it might cause the Head to go down to the cellar, where Tom had himself been to carry food which he had taken from the school store-room for the hungry gangsters.

"Very well. I'll question you no more. I think I can trust you, Shale, but after last night's excitement with the police you ought to be asleep. I shall not excuse you from afternoon classes if you are going to waste your time like this. Go and get those filthy clothes off."

"Yes, thank you, sir!" Tom almost whooped with relief. At any other time Dr Lumley would have probed more deeply into the matter, but his mind was so occupied at the moment that he let thing slide.

Tom scuttled back to his study, and got his things changed. He was very sleepy, for he had been up all night with the police looking for the missing Jeff Barber, but the thought of resting simply did not occur to him.

He knew he would never rest until the gangsters were clear of the school. That afternoon workmen were coming to make some repairs in the cellar, and the crooks would be found if they did not move. They had arranged to move to the Doctor's summer-house during the lunch hour of the janitor and furnace-tender.

Tom watched from his window and presently saw old Jacobs, the janitor puffing at his pipe. He sighed with relief. That meant the Grizzlies could now sneak out and transfer their prisoner to the new hiding-place.

For the next half hour he waited tensely, expecting to hear an outburst of noise, even shooting, if the gangsters were sighted by anyone during their short move to the Doctor's garden. But at the end of that time there had been no uproar, and he concluded that the transfer had been made without a hitch.

His friends came from the classrooms to hear some more of the story of his overnight doings in the search of the missing boy, and in their company he forgot for the time being his wotties and strange career.

There was some more excitement during the lunch hour, when the report spread that Jeff Barber's father had arrived and was interviewing the Head. Tom got a glimpse of him climbing into his car a little later, and had some conscience twinges when he saw the worried look on the man's face.

Tom would have very much liked to have told Mr Barber that his son was safe and sound , but he dared not do so. He had arranged for the Grizzlies to shanghai Jeff Barber out of England for some months, and in a way he envied the lad. Barber would have lots of new experiences, and in any case he would have no worries. Some kind of punishment was what he deserved for what he had done, because Jeff had disgraced the school in more ways than one.

Afternoon school passed all too slowly for him, but the Form master was kind to him when he saw him yawning, for he knew Tom had been out with the police all night.

It was a very fine day for the time of the year, with a crisp nip in the air and the promise of frost that night. As there was still an hour of daylight some of the boys grabbed their football boots and started off for the practice field have some shooting. They persuaded Tom to come along with them, and one or two of them started bouncing and passing the ball to each other as they ran down the narrow lane alongside the high wall of the Head's garden.

"Stop that!" bawled Tom, "You know it's not allowed to kick a ball in the road. Stop it, Smith Minor, or—."

It was too late. Smith Minor had given a kick which was intended only to lob the ball across to his pal, but he had kicked so hard that it sailed over the wall and crashed down into the garden on the other side.

Consternation showed on their faces. It was unlikely that the Doctor was in his garden at that time of the afternoon, but it was their favourite practise ball, and they did not want to lose it.

"You young ass!" snorted Tom, itching to box the Third Former's ears, "Look what you've done now."

Smith Minor was a cheeky young cub. He looked with a grin at the wall.

"I'll soon get it back. Won't take me a jiffy to slip over there and grab it."

He was clawing at the wall, and heaving himself to the top, before it suddenly dawned on Tom that in the summer-house on the other side were the Grizzlies! He had for the moment clean forgotten that they had moved there from the cellar.

If the boy dropped over there he would very likely run upon the hidden gangsters.

With a roar he rushed in and grabbed Smith Minor by the legs, hauled him off the wall, and pushed him back amonst the others.

"Come down from there, you little idiot. If you break your leg I'll get blamed for it. I'd sooner get the ball myself."

And to the surprise of everyone the captain of the school shinned up to the top of the wall and dropped on the other side. If anyone had to encounter the Grizzlies it must be himself.

PART TWO.

THE CAPTURE OF STIEBEL.

It wa well he had made the change. From the summer-house came the strong smell of tobacco. The gangsters were smoking, and Smith Minor would cerainly have noted the fact if he had gone over there.

Tom grabbed the ball from the middle of some bushes, and then strode across to the summer-house. A vague figure loomed in the opening, and he caught a glimpe of steel in the man's hand.

"Hss-ss! It's the Chief," Tom muttered, "Stop that smoking. I can smell it all over the garden. Do you want to make trouble?"

Then without another word he threw the ball over the wall and scrambled up to rejoin the others on the other side. They looked on curiously, for he was very flushed and tight eyed. Little did they guess what he had on his mind, or how narrowly he had escaped what would for him been a disaster.

After that there was no more kicking of the ball in the road, and they settled down to some punting about on the field. But Tom's mind was not on the game. He put up a very poor show indeed, nd some of the boy whispered sbout it.

"Reckon Shale's sleepy after his night out, but it was sporting of him to go after that ball. He would have got in the dickens of a mess if the Doctor had nabbed him."

Darkness came all too slowly for Tom that night. During the night the gang were going to leave the neighbourhood of the school and smuggle their prisoner somewhere else. Tom found himself sitting in his room and straining his ears for the slightest sound. He had left his window open for this purpose,in spite of the bitter wind which now blew. Dick Seymour came in a little later and shivered.

"Brr-rr! What's the idea of sitting in a freezing room, Tom? Didn't know you'd become a fresh air fiend."

"I've got a bit of a headache. Expect I'm overtired," explained Tom Shale, and hoped Dick would cut his visit short, but his pal seemed to have no intention of doing that. He seated himself as far from the window as possible, and began to talk about one hundred and one things.

It was hard to pay attention to what he said and to listen to what was going on outside at the same time. More then once his attention strayed, andDick was not slow to notice it.

"Your nervy tonight, old son. What's happened to you? Don't think your going to be kidnapped like Barber, do you?

"No, you ass, I'm just tired. I'm going to turn to pretty early," replied the captain of the school as casually as he could, "I—. what's that?"

He was on his feet and across at the window in an instant. Dick followed more leisurely, with a grin on his face.

It was a motorbike back-firing out on the road, that's all. What did you think it was –a shot? You've been reading too many detective yarns, you chump. Anyone would think this was Chicago with gangsters running around. Close the window and go to bed."

Tom tried not to look anxoius, but he was almost certain at the back of his mind that the noise had not come from a motorcycle. He had heard too many shots lately not to be able to tell one when it went off. Dick was wrong. A revolver had been fired somewhere near the road, and that could only mean one thing. The Grizzlies had got into trouble whilst making their getaway.

But he dared not rush out and see what was happening. There he had to remain and pretend to agree with Dick that it was a back-firing motorbike.

Half a minute later there came another. Crack! Crack!--followed by shouting and a tremendous uproar beyond the school gates. The voice of Todd, the lodge-keeper rose above all the rest.

Dick whipped round even quicker than Tom

"Gosh, you were right after all, Tom. Those were shots. Something has happened out there, and I'm going to see what it is."

They were not the only ones rushing out of the doors. Most of the boys had been waiiting for roll-call when the excitement had commenced, and now they were fighting with each other in order to be first outside. The masters had been further from the front of the building and had not heard.

Across the quad they raced, and at the gateway they stood spell-bound, for there was Todd struggling with a man who seemed to be getting the better of him, a man who wielded a revolver which still smoked.

Todd had the gun wrist tightly in his hand, and was keeping the gun pointed upwards. Crack! Another shot went offas the crowd arrived, and Todd gave a desparing glance behind him.

"Help! He's trying to shoot me. Help!"

Dick Seymour gave a growl, and without further hesitation hurled himself into the struggle. Half a dozen other boys followed his example, and within ten seconds the armed intruder disappeared under a pile of vengeful yelling youngsters.

Only Tom remained out of the fight, too horrified and spell-bound to move, for he had recognised the intruder as Nick Stiebel, one of the senior members of the Grizzlies.

Luckily, the revolver had been knocked from Stiebel's hand at the first onslaught, and no more shots were fired. The triumphant boys parted at last, and there was the gangster in their midst, looking in a very sorry plight, whilst half a dozen of the bigger boys held him.

Dr Lumley and two of the other masters arrived on the scene. Todd was gasping out his story.

"I thought I heard a noise, sir, and came to see if any of the young gentlemen were climbing over the wall. I was in time to see half a dozen men dropping from the wall to the other side. They had a heavy sack or something with them, and I rushed forward and grabbed the hindmost one. This was him. He drew a gun on me. I closed with him, and the gun went off several times without hitting me."

"What happened to the rest of them?" demanded someone, and there was a rush through the gate.

But the roadway was clear. The rest of the gang, with their prisoner, had escaped whilst Nick Stiebel was struggling with the lodge-keeper.

"The villian might have killed someone with this!" snapped Dr Lumley, looking in horror at the revolver which had been handed to him, "You did a very brave and foolish thing, Todd. This man is evidently one of the dangerous crowd who stole Barber from the police. Maybe now we have him we shall have a clue to the whole lot. Bring him over to the light, and we'll tie him before sending for the police. Mr Royce, perhaps you'll telephone to the town at once and tell the police what's happened."

The master so addressed hurried away, Nick Stiebel was dragged into the light, and for the first time came face to fave with Tom Shale.

His features had been battered, his nose was bleeding but his eyes gleamed out as viciously as ever. He looked straight at Tom, and there was something in his glare which Tom could not fail to understand.

The gangster was asking him for help. Nick Stiebel expected his Chief to aid him in his time of need.

Up until then Tom had been almost too horrified to stir. He had feared that some of the boys, some of his own chums, might get shot by the gangster. Now that the tables were turned a new difficulty beset him. Stiebel was caught, and the police would soon be taking him away. One of two things would happen. Either the gang would stage a rescue and shoot up the small force of local police in order to save their leader, or else they would desert Stiebel and he would in his turn give them away out of spite. If he did this he would bring Tom into it.

In either case Tom was bound to suffer, but it would be worst of all for him if the unarmed police got shot down by the rest of the gang. Whatever happened he must prevent that.

It suddenly occurred to him that he could do this in one way—by rescuing Nick Stiebel himself, and taking care that there was no bloodshed.

No sooner had he made the decision than he looked straight at Stiebel again, gave a nod, and at the same time raised his finger to his lips. Nobody saw him do this, for all were staring at the prisoner. Nick Stiebel lowered his eyelids for a second to show that he understood, and then turned away.

Doctor Lumley was questioning the prisoner.

"Now, my man, who are you and what were you doing here with your friends? He demanded.

Nick's eyes fastened on the Doctor's grave face.

"We came to kidnap you," he said ,gravely.

Doctor Lumley jumped.

"Me! You ruffian what do you mean? What were you going to kidnap me for?

"Well you see," drawled Nick Stiebel, still held by the youngsters who had made themselves his bodyguard, "My pals and I had a little argument about the date William the Conquerer landed in England. We had a bet on it, and someone said the best way to decide was to kidnap the cleverest man in these parts. Naturally that was Dr Lumley of St Ardens School, so we cameup to kidnap you to find out the truth about the date, and then—."

A yell of laughter rang out from the quicker witted amonst the youngsters. They realised that the gangster was pulling the Head's leg.

Dr Lumley went red, and swung on his heel.

"Tie the ruffian up and lock him in Todd's back room until the police arrive. Search him to see he has no more weapons on him."

Nobody noticed that Tom Shale had slipped away to the school again. Tom had work on hand, and he had to make certain preperations.

Unseen by anyone, he re-entered the school and made his way to his own study. There he unlocked his box and took out something which was carefully wrapped in a sock. It was the automatic pistol the gang had once forced him to accept.

PART THREE.

THE MAN-HUNT.

Todd's back room was only partly furnished, for he lived in the lodge alone and had no need for all the building. Now he and several of the boys were making a job of roping Stiebel to a heavy kitchen chair, and judging by the knots they were using, and the twists they were giving the ropes, he would have to be a magician to get free again.

The masters were ordering the rest of the schoolboys back to the building. The police would be there in five minutes, and so far as St Ardens was concerned the night's excitement was over.

But through the shrubbery at the side of the house crept a cloaked figure. Tom Shale had taken one of the master's black gowns from the common room and had draped it over his head and shoulders, leaving a couple of slits for his eyes. In this he looked sinister enough, but in his hand was the automatic pistol, and he had deliberatly changed his walk to a cat-like glid.

Nobody saw him work his wa round behind the lodge. The first notice anybody had of his presence was when a few seconds later, the door of that small room crashed inwards.

Todd and the four boys with him, including Dick Seymour, turned with a jerk, and their jaws dropped when they saw the black cloaked figure with the leveled revolver.

"Stop where you are!" growled Tom, as huskily as he could, "The first man who tries to bolt from the room gets a bullet. Hands up the lot of you!"

It was laughable to see the faces of the five who gaped at him. Dick Seymour had gone red. Todd had gone white, and five pairs of hands rose as one.

"You can lower yours," snarled the cloaked figure to the lodge-keeper, "Have you got a knive?"

"Yes s-sir!" gasped Todd.

"Then cut those ropes. Cut that man free as quickly as you can, and if he's not loose by the time I've counted ten I'll plug you."

Todd nearly fell over himself in his eagerness to snatch a knife and cut the ropes. The glaring boys in the background were forced to stand there and watch their handiwork being destroyed.

Dick Seymour's hands were clenched, and by the way he glanced at a nearby chair Tom knew his pal thought of snatching it up and hurling it at the door.

"Iwouldn't if I were you!" he growled to the boy, pointing his automatic straight at him, "I don't want to have to kill you."

Dick went white. He bit his teeth hard together, and Tom knew he was trying to master his temper. Of course, he would never have fired a shot anywhere near Dick, but the lad was not to know that. Tom cerainly had made his threat sound fierce enough.

Nick Stiebel was free, shaking aside the scrapes of cut rope. He lurched to his feet and stretched himself. He seemed about to say something to the group who had recently brought him into the room, but Tom's quick ears had heard the sound of a car on the hill outside.

That would be the police hurrying up from the village.

"Quick Nick!" he barked, "Get through the window. I'll hold them back. The cops are coming."

The gangster turned, picked up the chair and knocked out the window, and then scrambled through. The noise he made had been heard over in the quad, which was not yet clear. Someone shouted to know what was the matter, and Dick Seymour pluckily yelled back.

"Help! Help! He's escaping."

With a muttered growl Nick Stiebel snatched the gun from Tom's hand and pointed it through the window. Crack! Tom had only just been in time to grasp the man's wrist and turn it aside, or a bulletwould have gone through Dick's head.

"You blithering idiot!" he snarled, if you do anymore shooting I'll choke you till the police arrive. I've given you your chance. Now hop it! Over the wall and into the copse on the other side is the best way."

Stiebel became instantly meek. He had fired in the anger of the moment.

"Right Chief, you cerainly pulled that off well! Look after yourself. We'll give you the news as soon as we've got the kid safe and are in new quarters."

Over the wall he went like a great cat, dropped on the other side, and vanished fron Tom's sight.

The quad was now in an uproar. Dick's cry had been heard. Boys and masters alike were racing for the spot, and Ton Shale remembered he had to save himself.

Nick had taken the automatic with him. Off came the black gown and was rolled up in a bundle and stuffed under Tom's jacket. Then he ducked down and crept as swiftly as he could through the shade of the elm trees to the other end of the quad.

He could see flash lamps being used. Everyone was shouting with excitement. The St Arden boys did not have a man hunt every day, and in spite of their master's orders to keep back in case there was shooting, they pressed forward as eagerly as hounds in a chase.

Tom managed to reach the side door to the school again, had a narrow escape when some late comers almost blundered into him, and then went panting up the stairs to return the gown to the common room.

He succeeded, raced back again, and was in the quad as the excited searchers raised the cry.

"There's his footprints! He went that way."

Tom sidled into their midst, and presently found himself alongside Dick Seymour, who was about the keenest of the lot.

"Didn't anyone see which way he went, Dick?"

"Hello Tom, I've missed you the last ten minutes. Wondered where you'd got to. No nobody saw him. But they say only one dropped over the wall. The police are just arriving. They'll soon have the blighters, and a jolly good thing too. One of them tried to kill me. He plugged a bullet close to my head."

Dick was more thrilled than frightened. This would be an adventure to talk about for years to come, and Tom hoped he would never know that this near shave from death had been brought about by the boy he considered his best pal.

The police arrived and took charge. Some of them at once set off to scour the copse on the other side of the road, but Tom had not much fear of Nick Stiebel being captured now. He would have got through to the road on the other side or have slipped away across country.

The grounds of the school were searched thoroughly, but so many boys had trampled bout that there was no clues for the police. Naturally nobody was going to suspect that Tom Sale, the captain of the school, and now one of the foremost in the hunt, was actually the one who had rescued the prisoner and set him free.

If the pulses of the son of Scarface Shale were pounding a good deal faster than usual, there was nothing in his innocent face to give him away.

Tom had surprised even himself by his daring that night, but he felt he had done the right thing even though it had meant he had aided a criminal.

He had at least avoided bloodshed.

CHAPTER EIGHT.

ST ARDENS VERSUS LONGFORD.

The day when St Ardens played Longford Priory was always a big day in the football year, not only because it was always a keenly contested match, but because it was the furthest away engagment that Dr Lumley, the Headmaster allowed.

Longford Priory was on the outskirts of London, and the boys always enjoyed the long drive on the coach.

This year was no exception, and over ninety boys beside the first eleven piled into the three big coaches which came to collect them. St Ardens would not lack supporters on the rival ground.

The day was cold but crisp, and they bowled through the countryside at a great pace. If the youngsters could have had their way they would have asked the drivers to race against each other, but there were five masters present, as well as all the prefects, and any suggestion of this was sternly opposed.

Tom Shale, the captain of the school, travelled with the team in the first coach. He was in high spirits, for he had more reason than most of them for feeling light hearted when he was away from St Ardens. For a long time there had been a shadow over his life at the school, and even to be away in another district for one day seemed to lift this burden.

Nobody travelling in either of the coaches had the slightest suspicion of the strange double life their captain was leading. It seemed too utterly impossible to be true, and for the moment Tom himself forgot everything about it and thought of nothing but the forthcoming match and the tea which would follow it. The Longfordians always entertained them right royally.

The coaches swept through Staines, and on towards Richmond. They would soon be there now, and already the members of the team were beginning to feel the thrill of the coming match. Longford always turned out a strong team, and it would certainly be a hard fought game.

They arrived at last and were welcomed by their opponents. The players were soon getting into their kit in the dressing pavilion. The ground was going to be hard and fast, and the supporters were stamping their feet and clapping their hands to keep warm.

But they got warm enough a little later watching one of the most thrilling games they had ever seen. Tom Shale and his men found themselves up against a team every bit as good as themselves, and although he scored in the first ten minutes the Longfordians soon equalised, and for the rest of the first half it was a hard fought ding-dong battle every minute of the game.

No more goals were scored, and the interval found the twenty-two men streaming off the field with faces the colour of tomatoes, and a keen desire for a rest. Each man looked forward to a hot drink and a brisk towelling.

Tom had been bothered with a nail which had worked up inside his boot. It was not hurting him very much, but he squatted down on a locker near the window to take it out, and as he did so found himself glancing idly across at the lane whiich fringed the field.

A certain number of outsiders had been attracted by the game, and were watching from the fence. Several cars had pulled up and their occupants were as interested as anyone there.

Tom Shale's eyes were drawn by a group of men from one car who stood at the gate, puffing their cigerettes and evidently enjoying the prospect of seeing the game renewed. There were four of them, and as he stood up after lacing his boot the captain of St Ardens turned pale.

He had recognised the tallest of them as he turned to point at the dressing-pavilion. There was no mistaking that tall, slim figure, and now that he came to look closer, the other three were also known to him.

The Grizzlies!

The tall man was Slim Dolman, one of the leaders, the other three were all members of the same gang of crooks. To an outsider there was nothing about their appearance to mark them from any other men, but Tom knew better. He knew they were the most desperate gang of scoudrels in Europe, and he knew this because he was their leader.

It was an amazing twist of fate which had led him into contact with crime. He had always believed that his father, Captain Shale, had some kind of business on the Continent, that explained his frequent visits over the English Channel.

Not until his father's sudden death in Paris had the boy learned that his father was no other than Scarface Shale, the leader of this notorious gang, and that he had been killed by the shot of a Paris policeman whilst leading a raid on a jeweller's store.

Tom had been shocked, but that was not the worst of it. The gang had hunted him up, and had told him he must become their leader in succession to his father, for otherwise they were likely to quarrel about the choice of a commander. When he refused they had assured him that they would kill him and broadcast the story of his father's position if he did not change his mind.

The youngster had been forced to agree, but he had secretly promised himself that if they made him lead them they would get no profit out of it. He would lead them for his own ends alone.

So far he had managed to do this, although they had no suspicion that he was not heart and soul with them. Recently Jeff Barber, one of St Ardens boys, had almost stumbled upon Tom's secret, and the gang had promptly kidnapped him and shanghied him abroad to preserve the secret of their leader. Since they had left with Barber, the captain of St Ardens had niether seen or heard anything of them and he had almost hoped that they had gone abroad.

Therefore it came as a great shock to him to see that the group were stopping in the lane. Undoubtedly they had seen the school caps and recognised them. That was why they had stopped.

The colour came back to his cheeks a few moments later. Dick Seymour and Mr Gorden, the science master, were coming towards him. He dared not show any of his feelings.

"Shale, we've been talking it over with the other fellows and they suggest that we go all out for the first ten minutes to see if that will burst up the Longford men and put them off their game. They're cerainly the toughest team that they've ever put up against us. What do you think?"

Poor Tom had to give his opinion while he was more occupied thinking about the group of gangsters in the lane. It was hard to place the game foremost in his mind now.

It was the same when they were out and in the heat of the battle again. He was conscious all the time of those eyes on him from the gateway. Twice he missed passes, and flushed at the astonished glances of his team mates. Once he missed a shot which at ordinary times would have put his team one ahead.

Whispers ran round the watching boys.

"What's happened to old Shale? He's going to pieces. What's the matter with him?"

They little knew the suspence he was in, or that he had seen the four men at the gate nudge each other as soon as he had appeared. He pulled himself together after a while, and made up for his previous losses by sending Dick a beautiful pass right in front of the Longford goal.

Dick was not slow in taking advantage. The shot he sent in just touched the underside of the bar, and was going so fast that the goalkeeper had no chance of stopping it with his fingertips.

That put St Ardens one ahead, and the cheer could have been heard in Richmond. But their rivals were not beaten. The frenzied attack they launched kept the visitors on their toes all the time. Even Tom forgot his troubles and those four pairs of hard eyes.

There was some wild kicking during the next ten minutes, for everyone had got worked up to a fever-pitch. Once the ball went out over the line and struck the gate where the Grizzlies stood. It was Slim Dolman who tossed it back to Tom Shale, and the boy imagined he got a wink and a nod at the same time.

Did that mean that the Grizzlies wanted to communicate with him? Had they got some reason to give him a message? It was well that the game ended quite soon after that, for he could think of nothing else but the possibility of being drawn into some fresh scheme outside the law. How could he dodge them?

The game ended with St Ardens still one ahead, but their hosts took it in sporting spirit, and after the teams had bathed and changed there was the usual big spread in the large common room.

Tom kept in the middle of the crowd all the time. At least the gangsters could not get a message to him when he was surrounded by the other boys.

PART TWO.

TAKEN FOR A RIDE.

It was well after dark when the St Ardens crowd collected, answered their names, and prepared for the return trip. The coaches should have been waiting in the drive, but instead of being there there was a very worried driver.

He reported that there had been some strange happenings.

"While my mates and me were having tea someone meddled with the coaches," he said, "The starters are all busted up. Not one of the coaches will start. We'll have to send to London for spares, and as it's Saturday evening it won't be easy to get them."

"Someone tampered with the starters?" demanded the St Ardens masters, "Just what do you mean? Has this been done on purpose?"

The driver assured them that this was so. Someone who understood their job had deliberatly taken tools and wrecked the most important part, making the coaches useless.

It was amazing. The news spread like wild-fire, and the boys clamoured round the damaged vehicles, wondering who on earth had done this thing, but at the same time looking upon it rather as a lark. What was the idea of this silly joke? What could anyone gain by it? Those were the questions asked on all sides.

The St Ardens crowd looked like being marooned forty miles from their school. Hurried phone calls passed between the two schools, and Dr Lumley sent word that if coaches could not be found, enough taxis and private cars were to be hired to get them back.

A general call was sent out for cars, and a good many people living in the neighbourhood hearing of the boys plight, kindly volunteered their help.

Over twenty vehicles in all lined up to take the hundred youngsters, and it came as no surprise to Tom Shale to see a big black car with Slim Dolman at the wheel, well to the front of the queue. Tom had already guessed that the Grizzlies were at the bottom of this attack on the coaches, and he was biting his lip with helpless rage.

What on earth were they planning? If they thought they were going to harm his school pals they had another thought coming. That was one thing they would never get his help for.

The boys were being divided up in groups, seniors and juniors, and Dolman cleverly arranged that he should be the one to take Tom and four of the younger boys. Tom did not dodge him, for he was anxious to know what the game was, and to stop it if he could.

The cars moved off one at a time, and Slim Dolman got away amonst the last. Tom was sitting beside him, the others being crowded in the back.

"Well!" he demanded, "What the game? If you fellows think I—."

"S—sh! Don't let the others hear you, Chief. We're not meaning any harm to the kids. It's only you we want, and we'll explain hings soon enough. Just sit tight, Chief, and leave it to us."

Tom swallowed hard. He was tired after the recent game, but he would have enjoyedpunching the head of the man responsible for this outrage all the same. It was past a joke to hold up a hundred boys in order to get a conversation with him. Even now they had not got him alone, and he could not see how they were going to do it.

He might have known they had made their plans thoroughly, and that theother three were not idle.

On a lonely part of the road, Slim Dolman'scar broke down. Tom guessed at once that the "breakdown" was a fake, but Dolman tinkered and tinkered for a long time before announcing that some fault made it impossible to go on.

"Looks as though there's a hodoo on cars tonight," he said, "I'm awful sorry. Those youngsters look dead tired."

The four boys in the back certainly were yawning their heads off, and they did not look very pleased with the prospect of a night in the car. However, just then another car came along, with two men in it, and Dolman stopped them and explained the position.

Tom was not surprised to see these two men were members of the gang, and he admired the way in which they said they could squeeze in four boys but no more. Slim Dolman settled everything very smoothly.

"Fine! Then you can take the four youngsters on. Tell the Headmaster that Tom Shale will be alright, and that I'll bring him on as soon as I get a man to come out froma garage to repair my car. As he's the captain of the school I guess Dr Lumley won't mind so much him being out a few hours later."

The motorists promised to deliver the message, and disappeared with the other four, leaving Tom and Slim Dolman together.

Slim Dolman stretched himself and yawned.

"What a trouble it is you still being at that fool school, Chief! We have got to go to no end of bother tp get you time off. Now you're free for the night. We can phone later and say repairs are taking longer than expected."

"But look here, what's the idea? I don't want a night away from the school, and you've got a confounded cheek to arrange matters like this without consulting me."

"Sorry, Chief," said the unabashed Dolman as he cooly switched on and started the big car in the direction of London, "We had no time to discuss it with you, and when we accidently recognised your school caps on the football field we jumped at the chance. We were on our way to St Ardens to try and get in touch with you. You'll be wanted before morning to stop the men quarrelling. They always do after a big scoop, and Scarface used to have to be firm with them."

"A big scoop! Just what is on the books?" demanded the amazed Tom, hardly yet realising he was being taken towards London.

Slim Dolman's voice took on an enthusiastic note.

"A great scheme. Nick Stiebel planned it all. There's a big reception being given at a Park Lane house tonight in honour of Sir James Gundle's daughter coming of age. It's a big dinner and dance. Over two hundred invitations have gone out, and there will be about two thousand pounds worth of jewellery being worn by the guests."

"Well!" demanded Tom, a chill creeping over his heart.

Nick's fixed things so that the gang take the place of the extra waiterssent in by the catering crowd who supply the refreshments. The whole affair is being rigged up venetian style, and uniforms and masks are being supplied for the waiters as well. They could not have fixed it better for us. We'll be on the spot all evening, and then just before midnight, when everyone is jolly and care-free, we'll out with our guns and hold up the whole crowd. Nick is arranging for a fast car to be ready to get us away with the loot."

Tom clutched hard at the arm rest of the seat. It was a cleverly planned scoop indeed, and the thought of being mixed up in such an affair simply horrified him. But how could he get out of it now that he had been almost kidnapped by the gang? How could he stop this daring raid from coming off without arousing the suspicions of the Grizzlies?

Stop it he would. He made up his mind about that.

"Where do I come in?" he asked.

You'll be along with us, Chief. We knew you wouldn't like to miss it. Scarface would have enjoyed it. Then after the getaway it's you who will divide the spoils so's there'll be no quarrelling. See!"

They were driving swiftly through the busy streets of the wwest end, and Tom ought to have been enjoying the rare chance of seeing the lights and traffic at the theatre hour, but instead of that he was hardly conscious of his surroudings at all.

His father would have enjoyed this daring attempt! Mention of his father always shrivelled up something within him. Tom was expected to act as Scarface would have acted.

Well he would, but not for the same reason. He would play his part, but only in order to be able to checkmate the gang and prevent them carrying out this crime.

The car turned up Shaftesbury Avenue, thence into a side street where the gang were meeting. Only the two members who were driving the schoolboys to St Ardens were missing.

PART THREE.

THE CROOKED WAITERS.

Tom felt like pinching himself. It seemed that he must be living in a dream. It was after ten o'clock, and he should have been in his bed down at St Ardens, tired and weary after his strenuous game that day.

Instead of that he was in a georgeous Park Lane ballroom, where a world famous orchestra was playing soft dance music, and eighty or ninety couples enjoyed themselves on the polished floor. It was one of the happiest scenes Tom had ever seen. Some of the wealthiest people in Britian were present, and the jewellery which flashed on all sides would have cost a king's ransom.

He was all a part of the scene, for he was dressed like a Venetian gondolier, like the rest of the waiters,and wore a mask. And he was busy rinning round with trays of drinks and snacks. It was amazing after the big dinner which they had only finished an hour ago that the guests could still find room for so much more.

"What a rare time the chaps would have at that refreshment counter," he thought as he glanced at the piled racks and dishes, "There's enough here to give the whole school a blow out."

Apart fron anything else, being a waiter was not a job he enjoyed. It was not his idea of a man's job, and he had never been cut out for one.

Tom had already disgraced himself as he had upset a glass of port over the glistening shirt front of an old Major, and he had narrowly escaped shooting a strawberry ice down the back of a stout lady.

Those had been bad moments for him, but he was not the only one who had made mistakes that night. The rest of the extra waiters were all as clumsy as himself, because the Grizzlies had never trained for such a thing.

They were doing their best, and so far there had been no serious disaster to give them away, but the thought of there being a dazen armed crooks amongst this happy, laughing crowd of men and women was not a pleasant one for Tom.

When the moment came for the hold-up, the lights were put out by one of their number in the cellar, flash lamps were to be produced and shone upon the startled dancers by each of the gang, and a few shots were to be fired over the heads to make them realise that the Grizzlies meant business.

Tom knew very well that there would be bloodshed. Someone would resist, or someone would try to run, and there would be a tragedy.

"I've got to stop it, or I'll be responsible," he told himself, "I've got to find a way."

Eleven o'clock found him still trotting round with trays, getting more anxcious than ever. The dance was now in full swing, and evryone appeared to be enjoying himself.

Nick Stiebel was unmistakable in spite of his mask. He was the member of the gang whom Tom liked the least, and now as he passed with a laden tray of sandwitches he whispered.

"Only another fifty-five minutes, Chief. It's going to be a rare killing. We'll make the biggest scoop of our lives."

He passed on and Tom in his anxiety collided with a woman, appologised, stepped back hastily on to the foot of another, and bolted to avoid doing more damage.

"—fine show, but the clumsiest lot of waiters I've ever set eyes on," he heard someone growl.

Not much more than three-quarters of an hour remained for him to find a way to prevent the raid coming off. It was no good him sneaking out and phoning the police. For one thing he would never reach the phone alone, for he was being watched by all the rest of the gang in case he had any orders to give.

It was useless for him to try and scare them by pretending he had discovered a lot of plain clothes police amongst the guests, although he played with that idea for quite a while.

Niether was it much good him firing off a shot and trying to break up the party that way. There was so much noise that it would hardly be heard and the gang would think it suspicious that he had done such a foolish thing.

Then he absently-mindedly put his foot on a cigerette-end that some careless dancer had tossed aside, an idea came to him like a flash.

He grinned under his mask, and cast a look of triumph at the nearest of the gang who happened to be passing.

The man caught the gleam of his eyes through the mask and sidled over.

"We'll soon be waiting for you to give the signal, Chief."

So he was expected to give the signal to start the hold-up! He had not realised that before. Well if he had his way there would be no need for any signal as there would be no hold-up.

Someone touched him on the shoulder, it was the head waiter, a genuine one from the catering firm.

"Hey, you don't stand there mooning. Collect all the empty glasses and take them out to the kitchen. Look sharp about it, then come back with a tray for these sandwitches."

For the next ten minutes Tom was kept hustling around on these sotrt of jobs, and the head-waiter had no idea of thefury that smouldered behind Tom's mask at being forced to delay his own plans in this manner.

Niether did the guests realise when they gave him orders that he was trying to plan to save them being robbed and perhaps murdered. All they worried about was whether their drinks or ices came quickly enough.

But at last he had five minutes to himself and he slipped away to the far end of the great hall where some settees had been fitted up in recesses for the dancers who wanted to rest and smoke.

Under guise of collecting used glasses it was easy for him to discover an unoccupied recess and once there he swiftly got busy.

He crumpled up some grease-proof paper which he had removed from sandwitches, placed it on the corner of the carpet near some hanging curtains, added the contents of two or three boxes of matches to it, and then tip-toed cautiously to the curtained entrance.

Nobody was looking.

Everything went on as before.

It was twenty minutes to twelve.

Back he went, struck a match and applied it to the pile. The paper flared, the loose matches caught and flamed up, and the leaping tongues of fire reached the hanging curtains.

In a few seconds a sheet of flame ran up the wall. Tom Shale hurried out of the recess and backed to a corner some distance away. He waited for the discovery to be made.

The flames quickly spread.

The curtains caught the panelled wall and some overhead decorations went up like tinder. A great gust of smoke came rolling out into the ballroom, and a score of people saw it at once.

There was no need for Tom to give the alarm. Screams from frightened women and hoarse shouts from the men informed the rest of the crowd that something was happening.

Fire! Fire!

The cry rose above the orchestra, which gallantly went on playing in an effort to calm things down. But the dancers left the floor and fled for the exits, of which there where many, whilst waiters and some of the household staff dashed to see what they could do with fire-extinguishers.

The noise was deafening. Two hundred people made all the haste to get outside, and women snatched up each others wraps and donned them in mistake. Someone was shouting for them to keep cool as there was no danger. Actually this was the truth, for there were so many exits that everyone could easily escape. But with smoke and sparksflying about, there was little readiness to appreciate this fact.

Something like panic rose, and the flor was dotted with dance shoes and fans dropped by their owners in their haste.

Someone blundered into Tom. It was Nick Stiebel, his eyes gleaming through the slits in his mask. He had half a necklace in his hand and had evidently pcked it up.

"Off all the foul luck! Can you beat it? If that fire had held off another twenty minutes we'd have won out. There must be a hoodoo on us these days."

A rush of departing guests seperated Tom from the gangster.

CHAPTER NINE.

PART ONE.

A MYSTERY ATTACK.

The clang of fire bells, the whistles of the police and the excited clamour of the crowd, who poured from a mansion in Park Lane all combined to make an unforgettable din.

Tom Shale decided that it was time to go.

He knew perfectly well that the fire in the mansion was not dangerous, that it was mostly smoke but he was not supposed to know that, and it would have looked suspicious if he had remained cool and calm.

He made his way towards a side door, still wearing the Venetian fancy dress which was his uniform as a waiter at the ball that had been taking place at the mansion. Jostled and shoved in all directions, the youngster got into a narrow passage which led to the servants' quarters, and there something happened which was going to have important results in the future.

A burly man with elbows held high brushed against Tom and knocked the mask from his face. Tom did not mind very much, as the velvet mask was hot and stuffy. But a moment later he found himself pushed up against a tall man in similar garb to his own, and the man took one look at him before grabbing him.

"Hi! Your not a waiter. What's the game?"

Of course Tom was not a waiter, but he did not want this particular man to find out, for it was no other than the head waiter. The boy tried to struggle away and lose himself in the crowd, but just then a rush of people shot them both into the walled yard at the back, and the waiter was still clinging to him.

"I want to know what this is all about?" puffed the man, "Your not one of those I chose. Your a fake. What's it mean?"

There was just short of a thousand reasons why Tom Shale did not want to give explanations. If he had started explaining he would have landed himself in a rare mess.

It was true he was not one of the waiters chosen for this reception at Sir James Grundle's establishment, but niether were a dozen of the others who had worn masks that night.

The whole of the Grizzlies, a notorious gang of crooks whom the police of Europe, were so anxious to get their hands on, had been there. Tom had merely been one of twenty pretending to be waiters, but it would not have helped him to have explained why he, the captain of St Ardens school, should be amonst them.

It was all too strange to explain, and all part of the double life which Tom was being forced to live.

Everything had started when his father had died mysteriously in Paris. Following that the lad had learned to his horror that his father was no other than Scarface Shale, the leader of the Grizzlies. His father had been a crook and an adventurer. The gang had hunted up the boy, and told him he must take over the leadership to prevent the organisation from breaking up.

Tom had indignantly refused. How could he, a schoolboy, and the head of his school, get mixed up with a lot of crooks?

They had insisted. Unless he consented they were going to broadcast the truth about his father. Thus Tom had been forced to agree, but at the same time he had vowed that he would lead them in such a way that they would never get any profit out of their stunts.

That had happened this evening. The idea had been for the false waiters to suddenly hod up the guests at midnight and relieve them of their jewellery. Tom had been forced to take part, and there would have been a haul worth hundreds of thousands of pounds if he had not thought of starting a fire in a corner and so breaking up the party too soon.

But what was the use of trying to explain all this to a man like the head waiter? The fellow was clinging to him grimly, he evidently suspected something.

Tom did the only thing possible. He brought up his clenched into the pit of the man's stomach, and the waiter lurched backwards with a gasp.

Tom turned to bolt. Somewhere outside were cars waiting for the Grizzlies getaway. He would able to get a lift in one of these, and would make them take him back to St Ardens. Already the Headmaster of the school must be wondering what had happened to him.

But as the youngster turned to make for the gate a big hand shot out and grabbed him. He was jerked round to gaze into the red face of a policeman.

"No you don't! What's all this about?"

Tom's mouth opened and closed helplessly. This had torn it, and no mistake! The gasping head waiter had lurched forward and was pointing at him viciously.

"He's a fake. He's an imposter. He's dressed like one of our staff tonight but he's not one of us. I believe he started that fire. I saw him near the place at the time. You'd better arrest him."

The constable was peering closer at his prisoner. Tom would have struggled only he saw a sargeant coming up.

"An imposter is he? Then the chances are he's up to mischief, maybe a thief. He looks only a kid."

Tom took the plunge.

"Yes it was a joke," he gasped, "I borrowed the kit and took on the job for a joke. I haven't done anything wrong."

The constable's grip tightened. The sargeant loomed over them.

"Tell that yarn to the inspector at the station. Take him along, Jones, and see that he dosen't escape. There have been some funny things happening here tonight. That fire wasn't started accidently. They've made some discoveries inside."

something cold touched Tom's wrist, there was a click, and he looked down in horror to see that he was now handcuffed to the constable.

Handcuffed!

He nearly yelled with rage. This was something he had not expected.

The cold touch of the metal sent a shiver all through him. This meant the end. This meant he would be questioned and his identity discovered. The whole thing would come out, everything about the Grizzlies, his father, and the rest would come out.

The St Ardens boys would learn to their horror that their captain had been in with a gang of crooks and gunmen. His pals would turn from him in disgust. He would probably go to prison as fellow gangman of Nick Stiebel and the rest of the dangerous gang.

As in a dream he was led through the crowd. The constable signalled a taxi to draw alongside the kerb.

"In you get!"

Tom looked about him wildly. The policeman's hand was pressing him forward. A crowd was surging round to get a closer look at the prisoner, and suddenly in the middle of it he saw a face looking straight at him. It was the evil face of Nick Stiebel. The gangster was screwing up his mouth in a peculiar way and nodding his head.

What did that mean? There was no time to find out, for the policemangot impatient, shoved Tom inside, and slammed the door behind him as he sat down heavily.

The taxi-driver had been ordered to drive straight to New Scotland Yard, the very name made Tom shiver. It seemed like a dream. Only that afternoon he had been playing football for his school, and had had no other care in the World, now he wasbeing rushed towards police headquarters.

Once away from the crowd they turned into the park and made for Hyde Park Corner at top speed. There was the usual continuous stream of traffic n both directions, all moving pretty fast.

They were almost at the corner, and the taxi-driver had slowed to wait for the forward signal to be given him by the policeman on duty, when without any warning there was a roar, a big closed car sped up close alongside them, a door opened and two men leaned over and peered into the windows of the taxi.

One seemed to strike the taxi-driver, and the vehicle swerved. The other flung a crystal-like tube containing a liquid through the window of the taxi, and as an acrid stench swamped his lungs Tom Shale dimly recognised one of the Grizzlies. Then the world seemed to go black, and he knew no more.

PART TWO.

WANTED.

Water was being dashed over his face, and someone was speaking in his ear when he came back to consciencness.

He was in a fast car that was speeding along at a great pace. The car was packed, and he recognised the voice of Slim Dolman, another of the Grizzlies.

"Sorry we had to gas you as well,Chief, but it was the only way to settle that policeman. We didn't dare to shoot him full of lead for fear of hitting you as well, so we just dropped a gas-bomb into the taxi."

Tom bliinked and gulped. His memory was reurning. He remembered how he had been handcuffed to a policeman in a taxicab near Hyde Park Corner. Instinctively he looked down at his wrists. The handcuffs were not there.

Dolman laughed.

"We always carry keys for those things, Chief. We left them on the cop in the taxi. It's been a great chase, but we've shaken them off at last. We're nearly out of London now. In a few minutes we change cars. This one is known."

In a daze, the youngster realised that he had been rescued by the gang. No longer did the threat of Scotland Yard loom over him, but instead there was the kledge that he owed his freedom to these desperate men who did not hesitate to shoot on sight.

A few moments later they swerved into a side street, ran their car alongside the kerb, and were at once hailed by someone from a big cream-coloured limousine.

This was the relief car, and they piled into this without loss of time. When they were again speeding on their way, out towards Hounslow this time, Nick Stiebel growled from somewhere in the back.

"This was going to be our getaway after we'd scooped the pool. We'd have got clean away with a fortune but for that darned fire. Bad luck has dogged us ever since Scarface died."

So the younster forced himself to growl.

"I don't know what's come over you. When I first took over I you were chaps whoknew their jobs. Now I reckon your a bunch of bunglers. Can't imagine why my father ever put up with you!"

They muttered under their breath at that. Tom could not help grinning to himself at his own cheek, but he knew he had to bluff them somehow.

"It's bound to come out the other waiters being got out of the way," Tom went on, "You had all better lie low for a bit until the affair blows over. Now get me back to school or I'll be landing in fresh trouble."

There was some muttering, for it meant driving a good bit out of their way, but he insisted, and at two o'clock in the morning Tom came in sight of St Ardens.

The car stopped a few yardsfrom the gateway, he made his pretence of thanking someonefor their lift, and got a final growl from Nick Stiebel.

"We won't let you down on the next job,Chief. We'll let you know when it comes off."

The lodge-keeper had evidently been warned to keep awake in case Tom returned, and now he came hurrying towards the late youngster. The gang hurriedly drove away.

"Dr Lumley said you were to go to him as soon as you arrived, Master Shale," said the lodge-keeper, "Your later than expected."

Tom had changed back into his own clothes in the car, and now he went quite confidently to the Doctor. He had his tale cut and dried. The gang had arranged so cleverly for him to be seperated from the rest of the team after the recent football match that there was little the Head could say to him.

Just as he expected, the Doctor merely wanted to make sure he was safe.

Tom pretended that he was tremendously sleepy, and gladly made his escape to his own room. It would have given the Doctor the shock of his life if he had known where the lad had really been that night.

Tom was yawning as he undressed. His night's adventures had come on top of the strenuous football match with Longford, and he had every excuse for being tired. He did not even take the trouble to fold up his clothes, but threw them over a chair and tumbled into bed.

He knew no more until he was being shaken by Dick Seymour the next morning.

"Come on, old scout, the bell rang fifteen minutes ago! You'll hardly have time to dress. This is what comes of being out all night. Where did you get to?"

Tom started to explain. Telling the same story he had told Dr Lumley. He hated decieving his best pal, but there was nothing alse he could do. Everyone had to be decieved if he was to preserve his dreadful secret.

"Huh!" commented Dick, as he turned to the door at last, "We decided you'd fixed up with your motorist friend to take you to a London show. You were late enough. We—."

He paused, and with such suddenness that Tom looked up in surprise. His friend was staring at the chair where his clothes had been spread, and following the direction of his eyes, Tom saw what had attracted his pal's attention.

Trousers and jacket were Tom's regulation school clothes right enough, but the waistcoat was several shades lighter than his own. It was the wrong waistcoat. In the darkness of the car he had donned one belonging to one of the gangsters.

"Hello, you seem to have got someone else's vest, old chap. Wonder where you picked that up?"

Dick sounded surprised and rightly so. He was already reaching out for it when Tom snatched it from the chair.

"So I have! I must have taken one of Longford's fellow waistcoats. I didn't notice it in the bad light."

He had snatched it away in case Dick should look in the pockets and perhaps find something that would cause suspicion. There was no knowing what the waistcoat might contain if it belonged to one of the gang.

"That's about what happened," nodded Dick, but he looked at his chum so strangly when he went out that Tom knew he had not been believed.

"Phew, that was a close shave!" Tom felt himself go hot all over as soon as his friend had gone, "I must have left the other in the car, or did I ? where did I leave the blinking thing? They bundled the stuff about so much after we changed into the waiters' rig that it might be anywhere. I wonder whose it is?

He looked through the pockets, found a packet of cigarettes, and was about to toss the garment into his wardrobe when he felt something hard in the edge of lining.

He turned it up curiously, squeezed it a little, and out came sliding two queer little tools of shinning metal. They were as light as a feather, beautifully made, and of a shape Tom had never seen before.

His lips tightened.

"Someone's lock-picking tools, by the look of it. So they carry them in their waistcoat linings in case they get nabbed and want to get out of a cell or anywhere. Nice company I'm keeping I don't think."

He hid the tools away in the waistcoat again, and locked it in a drawer. He was still worried about his own missing garment, for he remembered that in one pocket he had scribbled notes about the forthcoming football matches, and his name was signed on them. If they fell into the wrong hands it might be awkward.

But there was no time to bother any more about the matter that morning. It was all he could do to get down to breakfast in time, and there were some special chemistry lessons which he took with a few of the seniors immediately afterwards that required their early presence. He had not even got to see a morning paper to discover whether there was any mention of the overnight occurrence in Hyde Park.

Several times during the morning he thought about the whole unpleasant matter, but his chemistry required most of his thoughts, and he tried to dismiss the Grizzlies and their affairs from his mind. Perhaps after the scare they had had overnight they might keep low for a while. He would do all he could to make them do so.

At eleven o'clock there was the usual interval, and it was during this that Reddy Trotter gave him a shock. He came up with an open newspaper.

"Gosh, this country gets more like America every day, Tom. Here's a stunt they tried in Park Lane last night. A dozen waiters were kidnapped and kept out of the way whilst a dozen crooks took their places at some big reception or other. The idea was to hold up the crowd and make a getaway with all the jewellery. A fire started somehow and that spoiled things for them, but they got one of the gang."

"They did!" said Tom, tryibg hard not to sound too interested.

"Yes, they caught one and were taking him to Scotland Yard when he was rescued by the rest of the gang slap in the middle of traffic near Hyde Park Corner. What a nerve! But they've got his full description. They'll get him again soon and—."

The bell tinkled for them to return to the laboratory, and Reddy hastily folded up the paper and put it on top of a locker.

Tom grabbed it as he went out, and a little later managed to get a chance of reading the description of the wanted gangster.

It was his own description in detail! The constable who had been in the taxi with him had had plenty of chances to observe his youthful charge. He was even referred to as the "boy bandit".

Tom was surprised that Reddy had not noticed the similarity, but realised that it was hardly likely that anyone from St Ardens would connect him with the affair.

The danger would come from outsiders, and from the police, who were not going to give up the search in a hurry.

PART THREE.

THE MYSTERY LETTER.

Three days of suspence had passed. Tom looked rather pale and drawn round the eyes. He had not slept very well on any of those nights. The thought of the police forces in Britain searching for a "boy bandit" answering exactly to his description was enough to disturb the sleepof anyone.

Every hour he had expected to be summoned to the Doctor's study to meet some detective who had tracked him down. In his imagination he went through a thousand times.

Then on the fourth morning there was a letter for him that he knew instinctively came from the Grizzlies. They had never written to him at the school through the post before, and he knew it must have been something of an extreme urgency which made them take this risk.

He sneaked away to a quiet corner and read it carefully, his heart pumping madly all the time.

"Dear Chief," it said, "You are in danger. The cops have got your description. Your waistcoat is missing from our car, and we are afraid it might have dropped out and been picked up. You've got to get out of the way for a bit. We're taking a trip to the Continent, and we want to take you along. It'll be wise for your health and everyone else as well. We'll fixit for you, so be ready and get your bags packed. Don't be surprised at anything that happens."

As usual it was unsigned. Tom mopped is brow, although it was a cool day.

They must be crazy to think he could get away and go abroad with them in the middle of the term. If he bolted from the school it would give everything away. What did the gang mean by fixing things? There was nothing they could do. If they tried anything they would only make things look more suspious for him.

Yet at the same time, if his description was being broadcast he ought to get out of the way for a time. The hunt would die down after a while.

The trouble was that he did not know where the gang had their present headquarters, so he could not communicate with them to warn them not to make any false moves.

In the middle of class that morning, the dreaded summons came.

"Shale, the Headmaster wants to see in his study."

Tom felt himself going hot and cold in turn. So it had happened at last. He had been discovered. The police were there, and he was being summoned to face them.

He felt that everyone was looking at him curiosly as he went out of the room. Did he show his guilt in his face so very much?

He hardly knew how he got along the corridor to the Doctor's room. It had never seemed so long and desolate. His knees were shaking under him when he neared the fatel door.

His hands trembled as he knocked.

"Come in!"

Somehow he got inside, and the Doctor's face looked up at him through a mist. Rather to Tom's surprise there was no one else in the room, or there did not appear to be. Did this mean that the detectives were hiding in a corner or somewhere to watch his face?

"Sit down, Shale!"

This was unusual, and even in the midst of his feelings of panic Tom noticed that the Doctor's voice was unusually kind. He sat down on the edge of a chair, and noticed that the Doctor held a telegram-form in his hand.

"Shale, I've bad news for you. I've had a wire to say that your Uncle James, your father's only surviving brother, is dangerously ill in Scotland. Your relatives have requested me to let you come and visit him at once, as apparently you are his sole heir and there is a lot of business to be settled if anything happens to him. I am sorry sbout this, Shale, for it was not long ago that you lost your father?"

"N-no, sir!"

Tom hardly knew whether he was on his head or his heels. The Head little knew what a shock he had given Tom, for to the best of Tom's knowledge he had no Uncle James, and certainly his father had not had a brother. The telegram was a fake, and in a flash he knew it was from the Grizzlies.

They were "fixing things" for him right enough, and their daring took away his breath.

"I take it you will want to leave at once, Shale. The telegram is from Edinburgh. You know your uncle's address there I presume? They have sent ten pounds by wire to cover your expences."

"Yes, sir I know the address. Which train do I catch, sir?"

"The one-thirty. They suggest this on the telegram. You must hurry and pack your bag, then get some lunch from the housekeeper. You must not miss it as it is so urgent. Again I must say how sorry I am, Shale. I only hope your uncle recovers, and that they do not keep you away from school very long."

"Thank you very much, sir."

Tom was outside again, making for his own room. His head was in a whirl. So this was why the letter had warned him to get his bag packed. His movements were being decided for him, and now he simply had to go or the Doctor would be suspiciousat his hardheartedness.

He set his teeth grimly. The net was closing around him. The Grizzlies hoped to have their young leader closer to them in the future. They were going to try and make another Scarface out of him. But he would fight to the last. They might be able to force him to pretend to be their leader, but beyond that they could not go.

He packed as in a dream, had his lunch, found himself telling his pals the story, and was soon on his way to the station.

As yet there was no sign of the Grizzlies, but he guessed that he was being watched.

Even at the station where he took a ticket for London there was no sign of them, and he sat back in the corner of his carriage and wondered if they intended meeting him at the terminus. Otherwise he would have no idea what to do, whether or not to go across and take a ticket for Scotland.

He need not have worried.

The station master's whistle had blown, the train was just starting, whhen the door of his compartment was flung open and a man leapt in and sat down opposite.

He removed his hat and threw it on the rack.

"Hello, Chief! You see we fixed it all right."

It was Slim Dolman.

CHAPTER TEN.

PART ONE.

THE ROBBED KING'S MESSENGER.

Tom Shale scowled at the man who had just sunk into the corner seat opposite him. The train was slowly pulling out of the station.

"You've got a nerve!" growled the captain of St Ardens School, "You were in the station all the time?"

The tall man grinned widely.

"Sure I was there, Chief. That was part of the scheme, but I didn't want to crash in until the last moment in case you had someone seeing you off. Now we are all set."

Tom Shale sighed.

"Well, and now what? he demanded, "Are we going to Scotland?"

"Scotland nothing! We're going striaght across to France. We told you in the letter that you've got to keep out of the way for a while. The cops are on your trail right enough but in a week or two the chase will have died down."

Cops! On his tail! Chase died down!

The words seemed utterly impossible to young Tom. Here he was, the respected captain of his school, being encouraged to go "on the run" by a gang of crooks. Sometimes he felt like pinching himself to see if he would wake up. Unfortunately he knew he was very much awake already.

The trouble had only begun after the death of his father. Tom had always believed that Captain Shale had some business on the Continent which caused him to make frequent trips over there. Not until after his father's death did he learn the gastly truth, Captain Shale was really Scarface Shale, the leader of the notorious "Grizzlies" a gang much wanted by the police of several countries.

There had been worse to follow. The gang had hunted out Tom and told him he had to take the leadership in succession to his father. When he had indignantly refused, they had not only threatened to kill him, but to broadcast his father's shame as well.

In the end Tom had agreed, but in his heart he had sworn he would lead them only for his own ends.

Now had come an unexpected development, when the police had got a clue to Tom, and were sending out a description of the wanted "gangster" that exactly fitted him. Nobody at the school noticed it, but the Grizzlies had decided that he ought to go away for a time. They had sent a wire to the Headmaster of St Ardens, pretending that Tom's uncle was very ill, and that he was wanted in Scotland urgently. That was how he had got away in the middle of the term.

He stared at Slim Dolman wonderingly.

"I can't go to France. I haven't even got a passport."

"That's a good one that is. Think we didn't arrange all that? We've got hundreds of passports all ready made out, and we have chosen one for you. Don't worry about that. We'll catch the evening boat train that goes by Dover and Calais. Before morning we'll be in Paris."

Paris! That was where his father had been shot by a policeman during an attempted raid on a jewel shop. Tom Shale somehow felt scared at the thought of going there with the Grizzlies. Into what kind of dealing might he not be led? So far he had managed to prevent them making any profits out of the raids they had attempted since his leadership had begun. He was not going to let them make a crook of him, but he had been clever enough not to let them see that he was working against them.

But had he?

The thought struck him that this might be a trap. Perhaps the Grizzlieshad found out his treachery to them, and were leading him somewhere to "put him on the spot."

tom squared his shoulders and decided he would face it. He did not lack courage. If the bust-up had to come he would see it through.

The train carried on towards London, and Slim told him something of the plans they had made for making their visit to France a profitable one. There was some talk of holding up a bank on the outskirts of Paris. Tom was inwardly horrified, but he pretended to be interested.

The gang had thought of everything. They had arranged for a wire to be sent from Scotland to the school on the morrow telling of his safe arrival. He realised that after that he could disappear and nobody would be any the wiser.

London at last.

They met several of the gang in one of their various headquarters, and he was supplied with a passport which they stated would do the trick, and which mentioned that he was a "Student."

"If you are asked why you are going over you just say you're going to study French," Nick Stiebel told him, and Tom felt the web closing tighter about him.

They were not together when they caught the boat-train from Victoria, but Slim travelled down with him, and once they were on the cross-Channel steamer he recognised several of the Grizzlies amonst the crowd. It was a very cold night, and there was a mist in the Channel. Most of the passengers were muffled up and remained below.

Tom Shale found it impossible to rest below. He wanted air, he wanted space in which to think, and he wanted to have a last glimpse of the British coast.

He found his way on deck alone, and trudged round to the leeward side, where he leaned against the rail and watched the water foaming by. The sea was fairly calm.

He had been there stationary for some minutes, not making a sound, when someone hurried past just behind him. He did not look round, but a couple of seconds later he heard a thud, a groan and a scuffle.

Whirling in shocked surprise, he was in time to see two men rising from the limp figure of a third who lay flat on the deck. They did not pause for a second, but darted round behind the nearest deckhouse and vanished.

"Hi!" called Tom , and was at the fallen man's side in a moment, "What's the matter, sir? Have they hurt you?"

The man was looking dazed, although he was evidently not very much hurt. He was well-dressed and keen-looking, but a gasp of horror escaped him when he put his hand inside his shirt and evidently discovered that something had gone.

"Theve got it."

Tom was inerested at once. He helped the other to his feet, and saw that he was quite a young man.

"Have they robbed you? Lost much? You'd better tell the captain at once," he suggested.

"No, no!" the man clutched his arm, looked sharply at him, and then said,

"You look an honest kid, so please do as I say. Don't say a word about this to anyone."

"But—."

"Please! You see I'm a King's messenger, and I had important dispatches on me. Those men who have robbed me are the agents of some foreign country. It is a terrible business that they should have got them, but publicity will be almost as bad. If I'm going to get them back I must work secretly, otherwise everything is lost. You may not understand, but sometimes it is necessary to get despatches across the Channel secretly."

Tom was thrilling in every nerve.

Dispatches! King's messemger!

He had been plunged at once into a real adventure.

If only he had been a few seconds quicker and had grappled with the men.

Then a brilliant idea came to him.

"Do you know what the men look like, sir?"

"No, but I suspect one is a fellow called Lityinoff. He may be disguised, but he will be tall and broad-shouldered, with a scar close to his ear on the right side of his face. He will hardly be able to disguise that. But there are eight hundred people on board tonight. It will be impossible to find him, or the dispatch wallet."

"What's that like?" Tom asked casually.

"A thin pigskin wallet about six inches square, royal blue in colour, with a snap lock on it."

Tom drew a deep breath, and pushed the astonished man aside.

"Don't worry, sir. I'll get it back for you before we reach Calais."

PART TWO.

TOM SHALE THE ACTOR.

Two minutes later Tom Shale was in the corner of the smoke room, beckoning to Nick Stiebel. He was surprised at himself for what he had promised but it was he not the leader of the best gang of crooks in Europe? Surely he could make some use of them.

Nick glided over to him, and a swift order came from Tom.

"Get the gang here. I've a job on hand."

Nick Stiebel's face flushed with excitement. He lowered his eyelids, and then grunted.

"Okay, Chief."

Tom sat down and pretended to read a newspaper. One by one the gang came in, and grouped themselves about him, some reading, some smoking. They looked just like ordinary travellers, and for the time being there were very few others in the smoke-room.

"Listen!" snapped Tom, as rapidly as he could, "There's a job to be done. On board there is a tall, dark man with a scar on the right side of his face, close to his ear. He's got a royal-blue pig-skin wallet in his possession. About six inches square. Get it!"

Some of the men began to rise at once. Nick Stiebel leaned forward greedily.

"What's in it, Chief?"

"Never mind about that now. Get it and bring it to me!" grunted Tom Shale, and that was seemingly the tone they liked to adopt, for away they went into the corridorsand passageways running from the smoke-room.

He glanced at his watch.

In another half hour they would be entering Calais harbour. Would there b enough time? It was going to be a close thing, but if the gang believed there was something worthwhile in the wallet they would do their best.

St Ardens seemed miles and miles away just now. The fellows would all be in their beds, some of them dreaming about Wednesday's match with Hangmere College. It seemed strange that he would not be playing for them, but he was playing a more desperate game than football now. Time drew on. People began to rise and rol up their travelling rugs as the lights of Calais came closer and closer.

Tom began to fidget and fret. Then he jumped. Nick Stiebel was right alongside him, and was tossing something into his lap.

"I believe you left that on the deck," he growled, and was gone before Tom could say a word.

He felt the wallet and glanced at it. It answered the description exactly. There seemed to be a wad of papers inside, and it was still locked.

He put it in his pocket and went in search of the King's messenger. The young man was leaning miserably against the rail close to the spot where the gangway would soon be run out.

Tom sidled up to him.

"Is this your wallet?"

The King's messenger simply snatched at it, his face flushed.

"Jove, yes, but how—?"

"I can't tell you how I got it, but here it is and I don't think it has been tampered with," grinned Tom.

"Jove, but—." The man seemed completely dazed by his good luck.

"You—you must be a magician. I shall never be able to thank you enough. You've done your country a good turn, and if ever you are in any trouble in Paris ask for Lonsdale Drew at the British Embassy. I'll do everything I can for you."

"That's all right," said Tom Shale, and drifted away, tingling with satisfaction. It was the first time that he had been pleased that he was the Chief of the Grizzlies.

What had happened to land the wallet in Nick Stiebel's possession he did not know or care. A few minutes later they handed over their landing tickets, and he was bundled down the gangway with Slim and one of the others on to French soil.

He was in France, the country where his father had died. How long would it be before he was back at St Ardens? Would he ever be there again? He found himself asking this question as he was bustled through the customs-house and then into the waiting Paris express.

The gang had booked their seats, and the compartment which Tom was, contained only members of their party. They filled it completely, and after the train started they were in high spirits. But it came as a shock to Tom when Nick Stiebel suddenly said to him.

"Well, what about it, Chief?"

"What about what?" asked the boy.

"What about the wallet? Aren't we going to see what's in it, and share out? You know the rules."

Tom Shale felt himself go cold. He had forgotten all about that, and that the gang would want their share of the procceeds. They had taken it for granted there was something of great valuein it, and they naturally wanted to see it.

He seemed to have got himself in a fine hole. He could not very well tell them he had been merely using them to do a King's messenger a good turn.

So he forced himself to grin.

"Don't be impatient, Nick. All in good time. You forget the ticket man hasn't been round yet. We don't want him barging in in the middle of it."

"That's right," muttered the others, "Don't be impatient, Nick."

But Tom was only playing for time. He was feverishly racking his brain for some way out. What could he do to explain his not having the wallet any longer? How could he excuse himself?"

He did not smoke, and grunted something about their cigerettes making the place stuffy, and stood out in the corridor to get a breather. He was under the eye of them all the time and he noticed that Nick was watching him keenly. Did Stiebel suspect something? He had always disliked him the most of all the Grizzlies.

He decided that desperate measures were the only ones possible. He was leaning backwards against the door of the compartment, and had his hands behind his back. Under cover of his body he pulled the door open and suddenly he let himself swing outwards on it.

But he took good care to be clinging on grimly, and when the rush of wind dashed the door back a second later he came tumbling into the corridor in a heap.

There was a cloud of smoke, a yell from the gangsters, and three or four grabbed and pulled him to safety at once.

"Phew, that was a close shave, Chief. What happened?"

there was no need for Tom to pretend to feel pale, he was white enough. It had not been pleasant swinging out there with the train roaring along at forty miles an hour.

He gasped something about the door having come open, and as the ticket-collector come along just then they all pitched into him and cursed the defective French door locks which came open when a passenger leaned on them.

But Tom assured them he was not hurt, dusted himself down, and sat in his corner, until his colour came back.

"If this is French comfort I'd rather be back at St Ardens!" he muttered. Then he braced himself up and seemed to pull himself together.

"Well, I'm lucky to be alive. Let's see what we've got in the lucky-bag. I heard that chap telling his friend that he wouldn't lose that wallet for ten thousand pounds, so I guessed it must be something of importance. I gave you chaps the wink because there wasn't much time, and because—gosh!"

He had been fumbling in his pocket as he spoke, and now he began feverishly diving into one pocket after another.

"What's the matter, Chief?" asked someone.

"It—it's gone. The wallet isn't here. Must have fallen out when I went through the door. It's back there on the line, and there might be ten thousand pounds in it!"

Tom had never acted better in all his life. He was on his feet, and looked almost ready to pull the communication cord to stop the train.

Growls of rage came from the gang, but what could they say? They could not very well blame their leader for the recent accident. Even Nick Stiebel could not point at that as being deliberate. They could only sympathise with him and curse their luck.

"Seems we lost or luck when your father died," muttered Nick, "We haven't had a scoop since then. We'v got to make up for it in Paris or we'll be going broke."

Thet began to work out more fully their scheme for holding up a certain bank they knew of in the Paris suburbs, and Tom congratulated himself upon having pulled the wool over their eyes once more.

PART THREE.

THE GANG'S GUEST.

In Paris they seperated into two parties, one going to a big hotel near the Place de l Concorde, and the other to a less well-known establishment. Tom was in the big hotel with Slim, Nick and some of the others. He had a feeling that their stay was supposed to combine business with pleasure. He knew that Nick was an experienced "cat-burgler" and he bit his lip at the thought of being forced to mix with such men.

But how could he escape them? He was more in their power in Paris than at school, for they had the money and knew the place, whereas he did not.

Yet at the same time, there was a certain thrill and excitement in being in a foreign capital. He ebjoyed hir first glimpse of Paris, and after they all had a sleep they showed him some of the sights.

Apparently their plans for the bank robbery would take some dats to arrange, and in the meantime they were willing to amuse themselves.

The first day passed pleasantly enough and Tom was very glad to get to bed soon after eleven. He lay there thinking awhile, and particularly wondering how he could prevent Slim from practising his confidence tricks on a certain rich American who was stopping at the same hotel.

This American had been "picked up" by Slim Dolman that evening and seemed to be rolling in money. Slim had winked at the others, and Tom knew that meant he saw in the other a suitable victim for his wiles. The man was such a simple looking soul that it hurt Tom to think of him being robbed.

He fell asleep trying to puzzle out how he could check Slim's plans, and he must have slept three hours.

Something wakened him about two in the morning, and he was surprised to feel a light on his face. He had the presence of mind to keep his eyes shut and his face still, the light moved away, but he could hear the rustle of clothing near to the bed.

His first idea was that one of the gang was in the room. Perhaps someone did not believe he had lost the wallet they had stolen for him, and had come secretly to search his things.

Tom got hot with anger at the thought, and lay there with clenched hands under the coverlet, waiting until the rustling was on the other side of the room. Then he opened his eyes and peeped.

A tall, rather stout figure leaned over the one bag he had brought from school. He grinned at that, the man would find very little there. Tom decided to let him get on with the search and satisfy himself. It did Tom no harm, and might check any suspicion the gang had.

So he lay there watching whilst the man carried out his task silently and effectively. The one puzzle was to guess which member of the gang it was. Tom did not recognise the build.

At last the other turned, and gave a grunt of disgust as he made for the window, which opened on to a small balcony.

As he passed through the window the light from some lamps below for a moment shone on his face, and Tom shot upright in bed in wonder. It was one of the Grizzlies at all, but the simple American whom Slim was going to try and rob!

The man had crouched there a while, and then seemed to pass along to the sill of the room next door. That was the room where Slim was sleeping.

"Well, I'm blowed!" muttered Tom, leaping from his bed, "That American isn't such a mug as they think. He's as good a cat-burgler as Nick Stiebel. What a lark!"

He was delightedat the turn of events. The gang was going to get stung for once. Instead of trapping an innocent traveller and fleecing him, they ha tackled someone in the same game as themselves. Bulliver, as his name was, seemed to be visiting each room in turn for something of value.

Tom crept to the window and was in time to see Bulliver vanish into Slim's bedroom. Not a sound betrayed his movements. Tom grinned again. He knew Slim had a diamond stick-pin he was very proud of. It would be funny in the morning to hear him complain that he had been robbed.

Then the grin abruptly died from Tom Shale's face. Another idea had struck him.

What if Bulliver was not a crook at all, nor a simple traveller, but a clever detective set the task of searching the bags of all those suspects? What if he was someone on the trail of the Grizzlies?

He might find evidence enough to satisfy him in Slim's baggage. In that case the police would arrive in the morning, and they would all be arrested, Tom as well.

The thought made him go cold. The gang would be sure to give him away as the son of Scarface, the man who had been shot in Paris by the police, and Tom could expect little mercy.

He must take no risks. He was in pyjamas, but without a second's hesitation he clambered over the rail of the balcony and scrambled along the narrow ledge. It reminded him of the way they used to get out of the Fourth Form dormitory a few years ago, but this time the consequences might be more serious, than a whacking forom Dr Lumley, the Head.

He reached the other window, peered over the sill, and saw a circle of light passing over Slim's luggage. Bulliver was up to his tricks, and he seemed to be taking more trouble. Perhaps it was because Slim's bag was locked, and the lock had to b picked.

Tom drew a deep breath, and suddenly plunged into the room, jerking up his arm.

"Hands up! I've got you covered."

There came two simultaneous gasps, one from the bed and the other from the man kneeling by the bags. Tom knew the switches in that room were the same as in his own, and he reached over and switched one on. The room was filled with light.

It was Bulliver right enough, and his eyes gleamed murderously at the boy. As the light came on he had seen that it was only a finger, and not a gun, which had been pointed at him.

He lurched from the floor and made a fierce rush at Tom.

"No you don't! Stop where you are."

It was Slim Dolman, this time ho had snarled the order, and there was a real gun in his fist. He always slept with one under the pillow, "What's this mean?"

"This man came to my room and searched my bag, and then he went to yours," said Tom, "I followed to see what he was doing, I believe he's a hotel-thief."

"Hotel-thief!" Slim rolled his eyes magnificently, "What a horrible thought! I treated the man, and thought he was my friend. The scoudrel! Ring the bell, and we'll hand him over to the hotel people."

Bulliver gave a groan. There was sweat on his forehead.

"Don't do that! Look here I haven't taken anything. I—I—give me another chance. Search me, and you'll see I haven't a thing. Let me go back to my room and I swear I'll leave the first thing in the morning."

Slim looked at Tom.

"I willing to give him a chance," he growled.

So, they searched Bulliver, found nothing and let him return along the balcony to his own room. Then Slim took Tom by the hand.

"Chief, your wide-awake all right! But for the love of Pete don't tell the boys anything about this in the morning. They'd never stop pulling my leg if they knew I took Bulliver for a soft one and he turned out to be a hotel-thief."

Tom promised, and went back to his room to sleep. He would not have slept so soundly if he had heard Bulliver take up his telephone in his bedroom and putting through a call to the headquarters of the Paris police.

"Yes, I believe it's the gang," he was saying, "I've got some evidence. I believe it is the gang who used to be led by Scarface Shale. Come over in the morning.

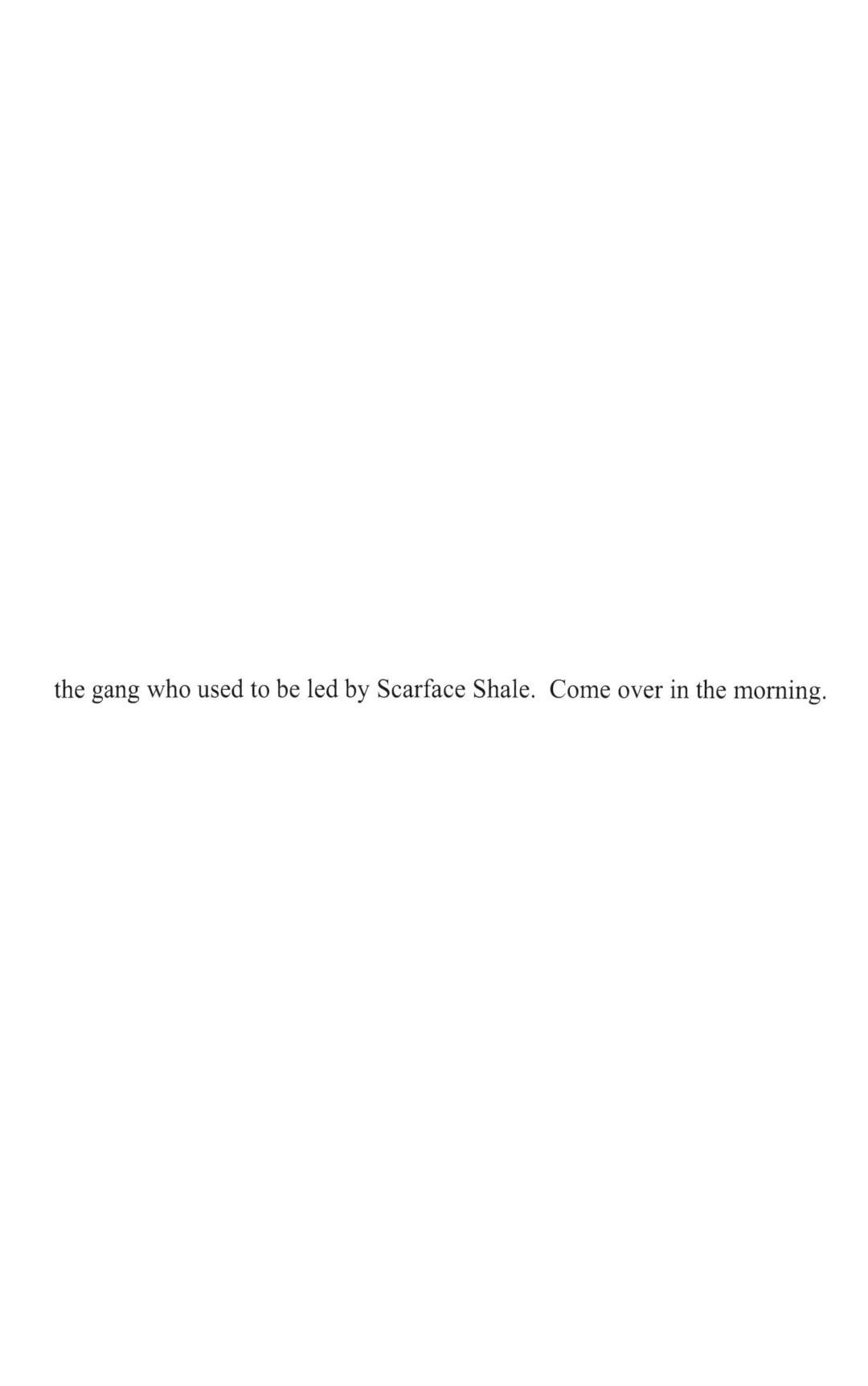

CHAPTER ELEVEN.

PART ONE.

THE COUNCIL OF WAR.

Tom Shale awakened and gazed from his window across the Place de la Concorde in Paris. He could hardly believe it was true that he was in the French capital, annd not back at St Ardens School in England.

But voices in the next room brought him back to realities. He was not only in Paris, but in company with a gang of crooks who called him their leader.

It was unbelievable, but it was the truth. He could hear Slim Dolman and two of the others discussing the overnight events, when a stranger had been found in Dolman's room ransacking his luggage.

That very day final arrangements were going to be made by the gang for the robbery of a big Paris bank. Unless Tom was very lucky or clever he was going to be mixed up in it.

The whole business had began with the death of his father in this very city. The news had come to Tom at school, where he was respected and liked by everyone as the captain. He had always believed that his father had a business of some kind that always took hi to the Continent. It had come as the shock of his life to learn that his father had really been Scarface Shale, the leader of the notorious Grizzlies, and that he that he had been shot by the French police.

Worse was to follow. The gang had quarrelled as to who should be their leader, and they had come to the boy and declared that he was to take over his father's place. When he had refused they had threatened not only to kill him, but to broadcast the story of his father's life.

Tom had been forced to accept,but had secretly made up his mind that they should never gain anything from his leadership, and that he would lead them only for his own ends.

So far he had managed to do this, but one or two things had slipped out about hisconnection with the gang, and they had decided it would be better for him to leave England for a time. They had cleverly managed to get him away in the middle of the term by sending a telegram which stated that his only uncle was dying.

Now he was supposed tobe in Scotland visiting his sick relation, and he was here in Paris instead.

He felt cornered. When he was at school with his friends and the everyday life as a background he had felt more capable of dealing with the gang. In Paris he was a stranger, knew nothing of the place, and had no friends. It was a desperate situation.

But what was that? He had been just about to turn from the window when he had glimpsed a couple of large cars stopping in front of the hotel, and from each had leapt nine or ten policemen. They seemed to have entered the hotel.

In an instant it dashed across his mind that all was not well. Had the French police in some way learned that part of the Grizzlies Gang was stopping there? Had his brief suspicion been right the previous night when he had wondered whether the mysterious person in Dolman's room was a detective and not a sneak-thief?

Luckily he had finished dressing, and he dashed at once for the communicating door leading to Dolman's room.

"Police are pouring into this hotel," he announced, "More than a dozen of them have just come in. maybe something is wrong."

Slim Dolman, Nick Stiebel and another man whirled at once.

"Someone has blown the gaff! We must get out quickly. There's not a moment to lose. Tell th others and make for the end of the corridor, Slim. There's a service hatch leading down to the basement. I saw it when we first came."

nick Stiebel could always be trusted to know the best getaway. Now the gang moved with the swiftness of trained soldiers. The six of them, two only partly dressed, but with their top-coats over them raced to the end of the corridor. They could hear the lift coming up and guessed it wasladen with police. Others would have been left outside the hotel, but it was doubtful whether they had yet had time to put a guard at the back as well.

The six men piled into the groaning service hatch, and down it went. It was used for baggage and such-like, and had it's finishing point in the basement. Coals were sometimes sent up by it to those rooms which had open fireplaces.

The captain of St Ardens found his heart thumping madly. He could see guns ready in the hands of the men about him, and he knew they would not hesitate to them.

If the police tried to stop them there would be a regular battle, and he would be in the thick of it.

It seemed unbelievable. If he was captured under such circumstances he would never have a chance of explaining. Maybe his fate was going to be the same as his father.

Bump!

They had arrived, and as they leapt out a startled floor-valet, wearing a green baize apron, came face to face with them. His mouth opened to shout his astonishment, when up came Slim's revolver butt, and the man went down in a huddled heap.

"Through the kitchens! There are doors on the other side."

Screams came from the kitchen-maids and grunts of astonishment from the chefs, when six stalwart figures with drawn guns leapt through the big kitchen.

"One shout from any of you, and we shoot you down!" shouted Stiebel in French.

Then they were in the sloping courtyard behind, where a van belonging to one of the big Paris supply firms had just pulled up with a load of foodstuffs for the hotel.

The startled driver was knocked aside. Stiebel leapt to the wheel with another gangster at his side, and the rest of them piled in on top of the groceries and other goods.

Crash! Crash! Thud!

Everything which got in the way was hurled over the tail of the van, then Slim Dolman dropped the canvas flap and away they went.

Hardly a minute had elapsed since they had left the hotel. Tom heard shouts, thought he heard a shot, and then the roar of the engine drowned everything. They were speeding down the byway at the back of the hotel.

He never forgot the drive that followed. Stiebel knew Paris as well as he knew London, and he turned in and out a maze of side streets at express speed without once touching any of the main roads.

Whether or not pursuit was taken up Tom could not tell but he never once saw a police car. Their getaway from the hotel must have been one of the cleanest and quickest on record.

They finally abandoned the van in a blind alley, and went by various ways to the place where the rest of the gang had been stopping.

Ther a council of war was held, and it was decided that in some way the Paris police had got wise to their being in the city. It was going to make things much more difficult in the looting of the bank.

Some of them wanted to give up the idea. Others, including Nick Stiebel, were all for carrying on with the plans.

"We haven't made a good rake-off since Scarface left us," he growled, "Every job we've taken on we've failed. I vote we go through with this and take more care than we have ever done. But what does the Chief say?"

A dozen heads were turned inquiringy towards the red-faced boy. Tom Shale itched to say he considered they ought to cancel the idea and get back to London, but he had learned how to play his part, and now he said as fiercely as he could—.

"Get on with it? Of course we ought to get on with it! Who says give up the idea? Nick is right! We haven't had a good clean-up since I took over. You'll all be thinking I've brought you bad luck if it goes on like this."

Nick Stiebel looked quite surprised at being backed up by their leader. He and Tom did not usually get on very well together.

"That settles it!" he said, "Tomorrow night we'll make the attempt, and tomorrow we'll lie low and get the finishing touches made to our preperations. The Chief himself will lead us this time, and if he has the luck of Scarface it ought to be the biggest we've yet done."

Tom Shale squirmed silently in his seat. Was he, the Captain of St Ardens, to lead a raid on a bank? If he did, and they were successful, he would be no better than they were.

PART TWO.

THE TELL-TALE LEADER.

The following day was a terrible one for him. The police had been combing Paris for the Grizzlies, and a full description of them all, including himself, was broadcast. But the Grizzlies knew Paris as well as any Parisian, and they hid themselves in the underworld as cleverly as possible.

The raid on the bank was to be made from the next-door building. This was a block of offices, some of them unoccupied, and one of the gang had secured admission by shutting himself in a cupboard when several of them had pretended to look over the offices with a view of taking one for a business firm. He had been left in there after the building was closed for the night, had taken impressions of the keys, and they could now get in and out whenever they liked.

It was the cellar which interested them, for they believed they could get from that into the cellar near the bank vaults. The previous night drills of the very latest type had been brought there. Tools and equipment had been hidden in the cellar, and when the time came they would only have to enter the office building and work swiftly and silently to burrow under the bank.

Tom was told everything. Any doubts they might have about his keenness had been set at rest after his outburst the previous day. Even Nick Stiebel thought Tom was as keen to get rich quickly as they were themselves. Tom rather encouraged the idea.

But in his own mind he had decide that the bank robbery should never be a success. In fact, he was beginning to work out a very daring plan.

He owed them no loyalty. They had forced the leadership upon him by cruelly threatening him about his father. It was up to him to defend himself and clear his life of their influence. He could never do this until they were under lock and key.

In England he had been afraid to get the police to help him because he guessed his own part in the affair would come out, and he would be ruined as reguards his school and his career.

In Paris things were different. Nobody except the gang knew he was there, and it ought to be possible for him to land them in the hands of the poice without himself getting captured. They were human wolves, and the only proper place for them was in prison.

He had racked his brains about it a good deal, and had remembered that he had just one friend in Paris.

On the steamer crossing the Channel a King's Messenger attached to the Embassy in Paris had been robbed of very important dispatches by a foreign agent. Tom had tricked his Grizzlies into getting this dispatch case back again, and Lonsdale Drew as te young Messenger was called, had told him that he would befriend him in any way he could as payment for what he had done.

"Maybe Drew can help me now," thought Tom, and found some excuse to get out alone for a short while.

In a cafe he wrote a note to Lonsdale Drew, reminding him of his promise to help him, and telling him of his trouble. He did not bring his father into the matter, or tell the whole story, but he told how he had been mixed up with a gang of crooks and how he wanted to escape from them.

He told of their plans for the night, named the bank, and asked Drew to inform the French police and advice them to set a trap.

He suggested that extra special precautions should be taken as the gangsters were desperate and would put up a fierce fight.

He stuck this in an envelope, looked around until he saw an urchin who looked intelligent and gave him five francs to take it to the British Embassy.

Then he went back to his own problem of deciding his own movements that night.

He did not intend to be trapped with the gang, that would do him no good. In some way he had to avoid capture, and if possible in a way that would not make the Grizzlies suspicious. If they thought he had given them away they would at once snitch on him to the police. But if they thought it was not his fault they would keep their mouths closed.

His hope that they would all be captured, and as they were "wanted" on so many charges he guessed they would be sentenced to long periods of inprisonment in far-away Devil's Island. By the time they came back he would have grwn into a man and be out of the way forever.

That was the plan Tom had worked out, and it was not a bad one for a boy who had never up till then had to grapple with anything more serious than the choosing of a football team.

The best thing was to get himself excused from the raid that night. It was not going to be an easy thing as he had promised to lead it in person.

"I must have an accident,"he decided.

That evening there ws great excitement in the gang headquarters. They were all keyed-up for the job in hand. They felt this was going to be an eventful night, and they were in high spirits.

Tom tried to behave as they expected him to behave, but he was inwardly quaking with nervourness. Would things go off as he had planned? Could he pull off the "accident" he had decided upon?

The time came at last for departure. Two cars had been brought to a certain spot, and they made their way towards these.

Tom was well to the front with Nick Stiebel and Dolman. Stiebel had taken quite a new liking to him since he had shown he was eager to lead the raid on the bank.

"Take the front car,Chief," he grunted, "Up you go!"

Tom ducked his head to enter, stepped on to the rather high running-board, then seemed to trip. His foot slipped, and he went heavily backwards, his foot doubling under him.

It wasvery well done, and th gangsters were completely decieved. When they carried him back to their headquarters he was pale as though with pain.

"Ricked my ankle! I put it out a football a month back, and it's gone again. Of all the filthy luck! Why did it have to be tonight?"

They expressed their sympathy, but it was clear that they wanted to get on with the job. When he had been propped up comfortably he gasped to Stiebel.

"Nick, you'll have to take over tonight. Looks as though I don't have my father's luck at all. You carry on, and don't waste time. We must stick to the programme we made out."

Nick Stiebel looked at him rather queerly, but presently Tom was left alone. The gang had gone to their cars and were on their way to the scene of the intended robbery.

He was tempted to leave at once, to make his way to the Gare du Nord, and make for England, but he knew there was a faint chance that one of the gangsters might come back with a last-minute report of their movements. If he was discovered to have cleared out when his ankle was supposed to be so bad, they would immediately be suspicious.

So he lay there with his leg before him, trying to be patient as he watched the clock and wondered what was happening at the bank.

Half an hour passed.

By this time they should be in the trap. He had heard enough of the methods of the Paris police to guess that the trap would be thorough one. If they managed it carefully there should be no lives lost.

Another half hour, and he decided he could safely leave. He was rather surprised that he had not heard some noise in the street, some newspaper cry or indication that there had been big excitement going on, but all had been quite normal, and he had concluded that this hd been because of the lateness of the hour.

He had just lurched to his feet, and was making for the door, when he heard a creak on the stairs outside.

As quick as a flash he slipped back and propped himself up as he hd been left.

The door opened and the grinning face of Slim Dolman appeared.

"Hello, Chief, all serene!" he muttered.

"Wh—what's that?"

"All serene! Everything went off fine. The boys are on their way by a roundabout route just in case we were spotted making our getaway. I don't think we were. There was no trouble at all, and nobody disturbed us. I've never had a softer job. Our drills simply ate into the vault as though it was butter. We must have cleared half a million francs."

Tom's head seemed to be buzzing. It was all he could do to murmour.

"No—no trouble of any kind? The police—."

"We didn't even see one. It was like taking candy from a kid. It's a shame you didn't come, Chief. But you didn't miss much. It was too tame to be interesting."

PART THREE.

THE PHANTOM ROBBERS.

Tom Shale lay back in his chair as though on a daze.

Had the British Embassy decided that they were being hoaxed and tore up his note, or had the little urchin just taken the note round the corner and thrown it away, keeping the five francs for nothing? There were two or three possibilities of that kind, but they had not occurred to Tom before.

He had to pretend to be overjoyed and full of congratulations. There had not been a single hitch and Nick Stiebel was rightly proud of what he had done.

That loot would have to go back to the bank, and it was up to Tom to find a way.

They were piling the table before him.

Mountains of notes crinkled in their hands, and their eyes sparkled at the sight of so much money.

"Your job is to divide it all, Chief. One tenth for yourself, and equal quantities for the rest of us."

Tom gulped.

Once it was distributed amonst a dozen different hands it would be impossible to get it back.

"I didn't take part in the raid," he said, "So tonight the leaders share goes to Nick. I'll take just an ordinary split, but I don't feel up to it tonight. There's no hurry. We haven't got to make a getaway. Tomorrow morning will do."

There was one or two growls at this, but he insisted, and in the end the notes were piled into a small trunk, locked up, and pushed into a corner behind his chair.

The house where they had their present headquarters was a big tenement building, and they had several rooms on one floor. It was a poor neighbourhood, and quite a number of bad characters lived there. It was this knowledge that gave Tom his next idea.

When the excitement was over the Grizzlies felt weary. Most of them curled up in odd corners to sleep, but in Tom's rom only Nick and Dolman remained. They intended keeping an eye on that money until the morning.

The lights were put out, and the door had been locked. The three of them were supposed to fall asleep, but Tom was certainly not in the mood for that, and he did not believe the other twoo were either. He rather fancied all three of them were lying there string at the corner where the box of money was.

Stealthily his hand went to the revolver that they insisted on him having. He had never used it yet, and had not expected to do so, but now he belieed the time had come.

Overhead there was a fanlight opening on to the roof for they were at the top of the house. Lying there on his back, Tom found himself gazing up at this lighter square. He had picked up a big rusty nail from the floor, and now with a deft twist of the wrist he hurled it with all his might at the glass of the fanlight.

He did not miss.

There was a crashing sound, but before the glass had even fallen Tom had leapt to his feet and was blazing away at the same spot.

Crack! Crack! Crack!

"Look out! Someone on the roof trying to get in. I saw two of them."

In an instant the other two occupants of the room were on their feet. Nick Stiebel reached for his matches, but Tom knocked them out of his hand.

"Don't be a fool! They might be armed. They'll shoot at a light. I'm going after them."

He grabbed a chair and pulled it beneath the fanlight. Just then the door burst open and some of the other gangsters came rushing in, guns in hand, all demanding to know what was the matter. The shots had alarmed everyone.

Tom had swung through the shattered fanlight and was on the roof, but of course there was nobody to chase, and he did not go very far. He went only as far as the nearest chimney stack, and crouched there.

Out came the gangsters. One by one they sprawled through onto the roof, and called his name. He said nothing, and made no sound.

They scattered over the roof in all directions. Down below there was a good deal of noise, for the shooting had alarmed the whole building.

Tom waited until he saw the way was clear, and then made for the fanlight again. In went his legs and he dropped boldly.

Thud!

He had landed upon someone who had been immediately below. Either Slim Dolman or Nick Stiebel had remained behind to watch over the trunk-load of money. His arrival had knocked the man flat, but someone grabbed his arm.

He felt the cold touch of a revolver, and knew it was Nick Stiebel who grappled with him. The light was poor, so poor that he could hardly see where the man's face was, but he made a good guess, drove up his knee with all his might, and heard the thud of it on a jaw-bone.

Stiebel went limp. His gun dropped to the floor, and Tom Shale scrambled up.

Tom seized hold of the trunk-load of money, and lifted it in his arms. It was too heavy to carry far, and he did not go any further than the corridor outside. With an effort he thrust it into a dirty cupboard which he had noticed and closed the door on it.

He believed nobody would think of looking in there for the loot. They would all think it had been carried off by the supposed thieves. Voices on the staircase told him that it was too late for him to escape that way.

He scrambled back into the room, saw Stiebel still stretched out on the floor, and got back through the fanlight on to the roof again.

Somewhere close by a police whistle blew, and he wondered what the boys of St Ardens would have thought if they had known their captain was up on the roofs of Paris at nearly two o'clock in the morning.

CHAPTER TWELVE.

PART ONE.

THE GRIZZLIES GETAWAY.

A dozen men scrambled over the roofs of a large block of tenement buildings just south of the River Seine in Paris. Guns were in their hands, and their expressions were angry.

Down in the streets the alarm had spread. Police and sight-seers were rushing to the scene.

The men on the roofof the big block of buildings were the Grizzlies, a gang of crooks who believed some other gang had just made an attempt to steal the loot they had gathered the previous night from a successful bank-robbery. They believed they had chased the intruders on to the that roof.

Amonst them, calling them by name, was Tom Shale, a young British schoolboy whom a strange fate had made their leader. Tom Shale was playing a dangerous part. It was he who had started the alarm and caused this chase on the roof, and he had his own very good reason.

The son of Captain Shale, he had always believed his father ran some business on the Continent. Not until Captain Shale's death did he learn that his father was Scarface Shale, a notorious gang-leader.

At the time Tom was at St Ardens, a famous English school, and was the captain of the Sixth Form. Worse was to follow, for the gang had come to him and told him he must take his father's place and lead them. He had refused, whereupon they had threatened him with death and to expose his father's career. So in the end Tom had consented, but had secretly promised himselfthat he would lead them for his own ends.

By a clever ruse they had got him to Paris in the middle of the term to take part in this robbery, and although he had not actually been present at the time, they had sooped a matter of over fifty thousand pounds. He was now doing his best to see that they did not keep this loot.

Behind a chimney stack he bumped into Slim Dolman.

"Got him!" he demanded, hoarsely, "I saw him double back towards the fanlight."

"We missed him, Chief," grunted the dandified member of the gang, "But if he went back there Nick would have got him. He's waiting inside."

"Then let's go and warn him," panted Tom, apparently anxious, and nobody could have guessed from his manner that he had already been back into the darkened room.

They scrambled for the fanlight which had let them out from the room below. Several of the others followed them, and Slim Dolman had no sooner dropped on hands and knees than he collided with someone on the floor.

"Nick! Where are you, Nick?"

he was calling the swarthy little man who was one of the most prominent member of the gang, but when a flash lamp was turned on it was revealed that Nick Stiebel lay senseless upon the floor, and that his assailant had vanished.

Tom Shale had closed and barricaded the door. The sounds of their shots had aroused the whole building, and there were heavy footsteps on the stairs as well as police whistlessounding in the road outside.

Nick Stiebel had shown signs of coming round, and they were propping him up as best they could. He blinked his eyes open, and Tom Shale was the first to ask.

"Who attacked you, Nick? What happened? Where did he go?"

The gangster scowled. Little did he guess that Tom's knee ached and throbbed through the violence of the blow he had recently given Nick, for it was Tom who had slipped back and layed him out.

"Dunno! Someone dropped from the fanlight on top of me. I hought it was one of you. He knocked me out before I could draw my gun."

"Then there's nothing to do but bolt over the roofs," commanded Tom, "Get that trunk of money and hoist it up. We'll be going before the police arrive."

Already there were voices outside the door, demanding to know what was happening.

The gangsters hastened to the corner where the trunk had been left, and the next moment howls of rage arose.

"It's gone! The money's gone. The guy who sloshed Nick must have taken it."

"What's that?"

The news revived Stiebel quicker than anything else could have done. He had been left specially on guard over that trunk. Fifty thousand pounds in French bank noteshad reposed in there.

"Gone! Then the swine must have taken it directly he knocked me out. After him boys. He can't get far with a load that weight."

Crash! Crash!

"Open this door in the name of the law!" came the angry bellow of the police-sargent who had been first up the stairs.

Tom grasped the arm of Nick Stiebel.

"No time now, Nick. We've got to make our getaway, or else finish in the French prison."

The short gangster muttered fiercely, but the others were with heir youthful leader. They were mad at the idea of loosing the loot, but it could have been worse still to lose their liberty as well.

There was a general rush for the table which had been pushed beneath the fanlight in the roof,and all scrambled safely out before the police had the door down.

Tom's pulse were racing.

So far his plan had worked perfectly. It was he who had moved the trunk of money after knocking Stiebel out, but he could not move it further than the cupboard out in the corridor. Ther he hoped it would be found by the police and restored to the bank.

Over the roofs they went. From the streets came shouts and yells of excitement. Slim Dolman was in the lead, and when they had lept a gap of six or seven feet with a penalty of a hundred foot drop if they slipped , they were on top of a building which had a fire escape at the rear.

Down this they went, and into a deserted street. The police were still searching the house and were right off the scent.

Down alley-ways and side-streets the Grizzlies made their way, and within ten minutes they were close to the Seine, where a line of barges was slowly moving out behind a tug.

The danger was over. They had once again escaped the Paris police, but they showed no joy because of that. Fifty thousand pounds had been in their hands only an hour ago. Now it had vanished.

"We'll go back when the police have left and try and get on the trail of the money," muttered Nick Stiebel.

Some of the others were more nervous. They knew Paris would be combed from end to end for them after this, and they wanted to get outside. Tom had already noticed the slowly moving barges, and now he pointed.

"What about a trip on those? They'll take us somewhere down the Seine."

His idea was accepted. The gangsters plunged in one by one and swam out to the barges. Some clambered out to one and some on to another.

Before long they were all aboard and slowly moving down the river, for the moment safe, but filled with black hatred of the supposed thieves who robbed them.

Tom had to look as gloomy as the rest, but it was difficult for him. He had done just what he had hoped to do, and it was up to him to prevent them from ever learning the truth. If they ever suspected he was playing a double life they would give him a cruel traitor's death

he lay back upon some piled sacks and felt the smooth motion of the barge as they lazily glided along. For the moment he was comfortable, and before long he slept soundly.

Paris, the gang, and even St Ardens and their prospects for the football season, were alike forgotten.

PART TWO.

TOM RESIGNS.

Dawn found them sheltering in a wood about twenty miles beyond the city. There was an old hut which gave them cover, and there they planned to stop until news came from Paris.

One of their number went off on a spying trip, stealing a ride on a passing lorry, and before the afternoon was through he was back again with the bad news.

The police had found the trunk containing the money taken from the bank. They're night's work had been for nothing. The loot had been recovered, and although the police had not mentioned where it had been found there was no doubt that it was in the house where they had been stopping.

At this news the gang seemed to see red. Blood-curdling were the threats they used towards the supposed culprets. They all seemed decided that it was the Apaches who lived in the same house who had done this, and Tom Shale could not help grinning to himself as he sat there and listened.

They asked his advice, and he pretended to be disgusted with the whole affair.

"If Nick had stuck to his job and had looked after the trunk better, this wouldn't have happened!" he said.

There was a chorus of approval from the Grizzlies. They wanted to blame someone, and they turned on Stiebel, and called him every name under the sun. Nick Stiebel was not the kind to take anything of that kind quietly. He lept up and confronted Tom with clenched fists.

"You darn little rat to talk to me like that!" he roared, "We ought to have left back in school learning the A.B.C. It was a crazy idea getting a school kid to boss us. We've had nothing but bad luck ever since you took Scarface's job. I've a good mind to plug you."

His gun had come out, and for a few seconds Tom looked at death at very close range, then the rest dragged Nick back and disarmed him.

Tom was pale but determined.

"Very well if you feel like that I won't keep the job any longer. I'll resign. I'll go back to school and keep my mouth closed. You can have who you like as a leader. You're a rotten lot of gangsters anyway. I'm finished."

There was a chorus of protests. Many of them now turned on Nick and told him he was a fool, and that he ought to appologise. Nick Stiebel had many faults, but he was very stubborn and he refused. Whereupon Tom declared his intention of keeping his threat to resign.

"I'm going back to school. I'd sooner face the chances of discovery there than be where I'm not wanted. I'm goin to catch a train to Boulogne and cross from there. So long."

His heart was thumping under his waistcoat.

He was quite expecting them to chase after him and tel him he could not walk out on them like that. He was afraid they would force him to remain, but they were so busy arguing and scrapping amonst themselves that they hardly heeded his going, and before many minutes had elapsed he had secured a free lift on a lorry going towards the nearest station.

He had only just enough French money on him, and he took a ticket as far as

London. It was a slow train to Boulogne, but once he had settled into the seat he heaved a sigh of relief.

He was free of the Grizzlies, at least for a time. Whether or not they would let him alone after this he could not tell, but they would find it hard to make him come backto them. He could always tell them that he and Nick would never get on, and that they must go without either himself or Nick Stiebel. He knew Stiebel was too valuable a member of the gang to be displaced.

The journey seemed endless, but finally he reached London, and sent a wire to Dr Lumley announcing his return from Scotland.

He had no baggage, but when he reached the station nearest St Ardens, and his two pals, Dick Seymour and Reddy Trotter were there to meet him, he was ready with a good story of having lost his baggage.

His chums were delighted to see him back, and after his first hour when he had to call on his immagination a great deal to satisfy Dr Lumley, he settled down again and felt that he had never been away. Those wild and exciting events which had occurred in Paris never seemed to have happened at all, and he found himself listening with great interest to Dick's account of last Wednesday's cross-country run. That seemed much more important.

The next morning he was back in class as usual, and he found it hard not to contradict Mr Jones, the geography master, when he said something about Paris which was obviously wrong. Little did the master know that he had sitting before him a boy who knew not only Paris but it's underworld as well.

That day, and the rest of the week, passed smoothly and peacefully. Tom really began to believe he had finished with his father's strange inheritance for ever. There was no news of the gang in the papers, and he decided that Nick Stiebel had taken command of them and be waging war on the Paris gangs, whom they believed to have robbed them.

Well, if that happened it would be a case of dog eat dog, and nobody would worry how many got killed on either side.

The following Saturday there was a trial foranother cross-country competition, and it took the form of a paper chase.

Tom and Dick volunteered to lay the trail, and they got away a good half hour the rest of the pack, which consisted of practically the whole school.

The ground was wet, but there was no rain, and as they strode along in running kit Tom could not help thinking how his last big run had been away from the Paris police. It was a pity he could not tell the story to Dick.

But it must be kept a secret. He had gone to enough trouble to do that already. Nobody must ever know about that chapter in his own father's life.

Dick knew of a swamp which was likely to make a serious obstacle for the pack,and as he knew the way across it they were soon picking there way skilfully through to a lane on the other side.

They paused at a gate in order to look back. They could not see far, but they heard voices in the distance.

"They've started, Tom. Time we got a move on."

A car had just turned into the lane, and was heading in the direction of the school. Mud-splattered and plastered as they were, they could hardly have been presentable sights, so they stood back to let it past.

Then just as it drew level someone hurriedly pulled down a window and said something to the driver. The car skidded to a standstill and a door opened.

Tom grabbed his pal's arm.

"Come on, Dick, they'll soon be on our tails! This way!"

He dashed across the lane and into a copse almost before his partner had got over the shock of so quick a start.

"Easy up, there's no need to burst our insides over it!" panted Dick, "We've got too good a startfor them to ever catch us. Go easy!"

But instead of that Tom was forging ahead, like a record-breaking sprinter. He had never set such a pace in a paper-chase before, and after he had lodged his protest and got no response Dick had just to settle down and try to hold the same speed.

Little did he know that Tom Shale was not running at that speed just because he felt energetic, or because he thought they were going to be overhauled, but because he had recognised Slim Dolman in the car and one or two of the other Grizzlies.

Slim had pointed at him and stopped the car. Tom had an idea the Grizzlies wanted to speak to him most urgently, and he was willing to run ten miles rather than meet them.

On and on he ran, scattering the trail rather more thinly than usual. They had planned to cut back to the main road and make a circle of about five miles, but Tom decided to avoid the main road and to extend the chase to seven miles.

Dick panted and grumbled, but he kept up pretty well, and not until they were entering one of the side gates into the school grounds did he voice his real thoughts.

"Of all the chumps! What's the idea of bursting ourselves like this just to lay a trail. They won't be back for another half hour or more, and they'll raise steam that you didn't stick to the route old Morley planned."

Tom was glancing back through the gat towards the road. He believed he saw the same car outside.

"Oh I felt energetic that's all. Does a chap good to stretch his legs sometimes. Now we've got a good time for a tub before the others arrive."

But in his heart he was wondering what on earth the Grizzlies wanted with him now? Had they come to force himto take up the leadership again? If so he would do all could to dodge the interview with them.

PART THREE.

THE KILLER.

Everyone was tired and a bit stiff that evening. It was cosy round the fires in the common rooms, and nobody minded the howling of the wind outside the windows, nobody except Tom Shale.

For some reason he was nervous and jumpy. The wind made him think of howling wolves, and wolves reminded him of those human wolves—the Grizzlies! Almost wished now that he had given Slim Dolman the chance of speaking to him, for he would have known the worst by then, but it would have been impossible with Dick there.

Dolman ought to have known that. Tom was rather surprised that he had stopped the car when he had seen the young Chief was not alone. It was not like Slim Dolman, who was one of the most sensible men in the gang.

The evening came to an end at last, and they all turned in. tom and the other prefects making the usual round of dormitories first.

His own room looked very secureand comfortable. He undressed and got between the sheets with a sigh of relief. Whatever was in store for him could be put off until the morrow, and he was determined that whtever they said or threatened the Grizzlies were not going to get him back.

But sleep did not come. For one thing the wind banged and rattled his window so much that he had to wedge it, and when he had returned to bed it was to hear a window at the end of the corridor rattling even worse than his.

"I can't stick this," thought Tom, a little later, and got out with a wad of paper to wedge that as well.

The corridor was in darkness, but the window was outlined clearly at the end. There was no needfor him to switch on the lights and risk rousing anyone else.

He padded softly along the passage with his bare feet, and had almost got to where another corridor went off to B Dormitory, when he was surprised to hear someone coming down that passage. Like himself they seemed to be without footwear, and were taking every precaution to avoid making a noise.

Tom was puzzled. It might be one of the masters sneeking around to see thateveryone was in bed, but that was unlikely. There was omly one or two who had that unpleasant habit.

"More likely it's one of the young cubs coming to give me a scare," he muttered, for the corridor led only to his room, "I'll give him the shock of his life."

He tip-toed back to his room door, where there was a recess, and where he flattened himself in the shadows, hardly daring to breathe.

The figure reached the junction of the corridor, and turned to the right. Tom smiled grimly. He would not interrupt just yet, but would let the youngster start whet he had come to do, and then grab him by the nape of the neck.

Stride by stride the figure drew nearer his door, and at last paused with one hand on the knob.

For the first time Tom got a shock. He expected a boy much shorter than himself, and this was someone far taller. He tried to rack his brains to think who it could be, and had not solved the problem when he saw the door opening inwards.

"Jove, whoever he is he knows how to open a door softly!" he thought,"So he's going inside!"

He craned forward to see what ws happening. The prowler had halted outside the room, and was outlined by a faint lightfrom the window. It was not a boy at all, but a man muffled in a high-necked jersey and wearing a cap pulled well down over his face.

One of his arms slowly raised and pointed at the bed in the corner, which was clear enough because of the white sheets and pillows.

Then Tom got the shock of his life. There came a flash, a report, another flash.

Crack! Crack! Crack! Crack!

Four shots in quick succession rang out, and as the fourth finished the man whirled and was of like a shot before Tom could gather his wits enough to grab him.

Too astonished even to start in pursuit at once, the captain of St Ardens was a good twenty paces behind when the man reached the top of the staircase and went down them like a goat down a mountainside. A few seconds later a door slammed. He had left the school.

Whee-ee-eeew! Went the wind, and the door slammed open again. A gust caught the window at the top of the stairs, and it bodily inwards frame and glass as well.

Tom was wrestling with the broken blind when Dr Lumley, two of the other masters and some of the boys came racing on the scene.

"What has happened, Shale? What was that noise? Who fired shots?"

Tom had done some quick thinking. He thanked his lucky stars they could not smell the gunpowder there as in his room.

"Shots, sir?" he echoed in surprise, "I heard a dreadful noise and rushed out. The window came in. the winds burst the door open from the quad at the bottom of the stairs. The draught must have slammed the door and smashed the window frame as well. I expect that was the noise you heard."

He waited anxiously. Would they believe him? Would that suggestion go down with the Head?

To his relief, Dr Lumley switched on the lights and surveyed the damage.

"Yes, it must have been that. I was in a sound sleep and awakened thinking there were shots. Very foolish of me I'm sure. Send those boys back to bed, Shale. We'll do what we can to board this up for the night and get someone to attend to it in the morning. See what is wrong with that door on your way down."

Tom did so, and discovered what he had expected, that the lock had been picked. He said nothing about that to anyone, but locked it again, chased the inquisitive boys back to bed, and then was himself ordered to return to his room.

"You have no slippers on!" thundered Dr Lumley, "You might catch your death of cold. Go back to your bed at once, Shale."

Back went Tom, but he did switch on the light until his door was closed and locked. Then he looked at his bed in the corner of the room, and he felt himself go hot and cold in turn.

In his pillow there were two bullet holes. Two others had gone through the mattress where his body usually lay curled.

There was no wonder he shivered. But for that banging window, and if he had not been out of his bed at the time, he would have been riddled as he slept.

One thing was certain. This business was no accident. Someone had deliberately broken into the school, sought out his room, and done their best to kill him.

Only one set of outsiders knew where his roomwas—the Grizzlies.

He remembered seeing Dolman and another in the car in the lane that afternoon. He had been right to be nervous at the time.

The gang were trying to put him "on the spot." That could only mean one thing. They had discovered that he had been working against them, and they were going to kill him as a traitor.

CHAPTER THIRTEEN.

PART ONE.

THE WARNING.

Tom Shale, the captain of St Ardens, had just escaped being murdered by the skin of his teeth. At this moment he was wondering by how little he had missed death.

A window in the corridor outside his bedroom had been rattling with the high wind. Tom had gone out to fasten it, and in doing so, had seen a sinister figure open his bedroom door and fire four shots in the direction of his bed.

Tom Shale had missed death by a hair's breadth, and now he realized that the Grizzlies were out to put him on the spot with a vengence.

As he removed the bullet-scarred pillow from his bed and turned back the sheet to try and find the two shots which had lodged in his mattress his heart was thumping madly.

Carefully he extracted the bullets and dropped them into a vase on top of a high bookcase. Then he deliberately put his finger through one of the bullet holes of the pillow and ripped the linen covering. He would rather get blamed for tearing his bedclothes than anyone in the school know that his life had been in danger that windy night.

For the Captain of St Ardens had a secret he meant to keep as long as possible. Nobody at the school knew he was the son of Scarface Shale, the notorious gang leader. Tom had not guessed it himself until after his father's death.

The gang had come to him and had told him the astonishing news. Furthermore, they had insisted that he should become their leader in succession to his father, and had threatened him with death and exposure if he refused.

For months Tom Shale had been carrying on the part of gang leader and schoolboy, but he had taken good care that they had never gained anything under his leadership. He had secretly worked against them whilst pretending to work for them.

Only a day or two before he had resigned the leadership after a quarrel with Nick Stiebel, and as they had all been quarreling and arguing at the time they had let him leave.

Now it seemed that they had found out something of what he had been doing to cause so many failures, and they had sent one their gunmen to wipe him out.

They had failed, but Tom wondered how long it would be before they made a second attempt.

He got back into bed and lay watching the window. He was in a terrible position, for he could take nobody into his confidence. His pakls at the school knew nothingof the life he had been leading. He could not go to the Headmaster, for Dr Lumley would undoubtedly turn away a gangster's son. He could not even go to the police, for they were alreadyafter someone with his description. It looked as though he must face his ordeal alone.

He knew the gunmen were utterly ruthless. He had seen many examples of their cruelty, and they would think no more of killing him thanof destroying a stray dog.

But Tom was really tired, and in spite of the excitement and shock soon fell asleep. Daylight was streaming in at the window, and the wind had subsided when he opened his eyes. Everything looked so ordinary and familiar that it was several minutes before the terrible recollection came to him. He was doomed to die!

Somehow he could not believe it! He dressed, washed, and was soon amongst the others, seeing that the younger ones filed into the breakfast hall. Surrounded by glowing, merry faces, with the dozen and one affairs of the day to be attended to, he found it hard to believe that the Grizzlies were after him.

What form would the next attempt on his life take? He glanced out of the window as he made for his place at the top of the table, and wondered if a long range shot would come in through there. Anyone sitting on top of the quad wall would able to see him and shoot.

Instinctively, he found himself edging away from the other boys so that he might not endanger them.

Then someone gave him a letter, and he nearly dropped it when he recognised the bold handwritting. It was from the Grizzlies.

It was short and straight to the point.

"We found out about that loot in Paris. You're a double traitor, and there's only one penalty for that—death."

There was no signature, but none was needed. They must have learned that he had escaped the previous night, and were already preparing for the next attempt.

Slap!

Someone banged him on the back, and he nearly jumped out of his skin.

"Hello, old chap! You look peaky this morning. Something scare you?"

It was only Dick Seymour, his special pal. Tom forced a grin.

"Scared me, no! I didn't sleep very well last night. I expect that's it. The window was blown in at the end of my corridor."

"Yes, so I heard. I'll bet it startled you."

Poor old Dick would have been startled himself if he had seen the note that lay at that moment in Tom's pocket.

Later they were in the classroom, for once Tom felt safe. Not even a bullet could reach him there, for they were high up from the ground level. He tried to relax his mind and forget what was threatening him. After all things like this did not happen in Britain! Surely there could be some way of getting out of it. The Grizzlies were powerful, but they were not unbeatable.

By mid-day, Tom had recovered his nerve. It was no use getting scared about it and going to pieces. He had stuck out everything so far, and he would see it through. He still had the gun which the gangsters had given him, and he would have carried it with him if it had not been too risky a thing to have done. A nice thing it would have been if he had pulled a six-shooter out in the Common Room along with his hankerchief!

One thing was certain. He was not going outside the school for a while. That would be asking for trouble. Dick and Reddy were going down to the football field for some gear during the lunch interval, and they had asked him to come with them. He had to make some excuse to remain behind.

"The truth is he tired himself out on that paper-chase yesterday!" grinned Dick, "He ran as though the police were after him. He's stiff today."

Tom let it go at that. He felt safer inside the walls of the school, and whilst he was waiting for the lunch bell to go he took a walk round the quad.

Thud!

Something had dropped almost at his feet, and he was so startled that he jumped back quite a couple of yards.

It was a small square package done up in string. It might have been a packet of a hundred cigarettes, it was about that size. Tom was about to go forward and pick it up when some inner instinct told him to be careful. He dodged behind one of the elm trees instead.

It was well he did so. The next moment there was a puff of smoke from it, a miniature explosion about as loud as that from a bursting toy balloon, and a cloud of green fumes spread out for some yards around the burst packet.

Tom backed away behind another tree, but even there a whiff of gas came to him and made him catch his breadth. For a moment it made everything go black, but he clutched at the tree and the feeling passed off. The gas slowly drifted away.

"Gosh!" muttered the youngster, "A gas-bomb. They saw me coming this way and threw it over for me to pick up. It was supposed to go off in my face."

As he stood there, rather pale and shakey, he heard a scraping on the outside of the quad wall. He knew what it was. Someone was about to climb up to see the result of their attempt.

Tom's eyes hardened, and he swiftly picked up a sizeable stone, stood close to the tree and waited.

A cap came over the top edge of the wall, followed by a pale , evil face, that of a Grizzlie known as Micky. Tom's hand came up and over, the stone flew swiftly, and there was a dull thud as it caught Micky between the eyes.

A howl of pain, and the gangster let go his hold and crashed backwards into the road on the other side. Tom heard a confused murmur of voices, and his eyes gleamed.

He'd show them he could hit back. If they thought they were going to have everything their own way they would be jolly well mistaken.

Then a couple of Second Form boys came round the corner, and he hastily kicked the little packet out of sight. He sauntered on, hearing as he went one of the two remarking to the other that there seemed to be "an awful stink of gas" somewhere.

PART TWO.

BESIEGED.

Tom Shale then knew that the school was being watched all the time. He was practically besieged at St Ardens. They meant to get him some way or other, and it was not heathly to know that there were murderers prowling round the buildings all the time.

He spoke to the lodge-keeper about seeing some suspicious-looking characters near the Doctor's garden, and the man promised to turn his bulldog loose that night.

Tom had no intention of going out that evening at all, but after tea he was asked to go to the station to meet one of the younger boys who had been away sick, and who was returning by train.

The Captain of the school could not very well refuse, he had no excuse for doing so. At any other time he would have welcomed the opportunity for a walk down to the station and a taxi ride back again. But inwardly he wondered whether this was his death sentence. If he went out there at dusk he was inviting a swift bullet.

He was tempted to ask Dick or Reddy to accompany him, but decided that that would hardly be the sporting thing to do. A shot meant for him might well hit one of his pals, and he knew he would never forgive himself if that happened.

He crammed his cap on his head and made for the gate. He coul not help glancing back at the old school, and towards the window of his room. Maybe it was the last time he would ever see it. It was a strange thought.

The gate-keeper said something about the rain keeping off, and then the son of Scarface Shale was in the road, feeling like a condemned man walking to the scaffold.

Being a cloudy evening it was getting dark very early, and as he trudged dow nthe lane, his fists clenched in his pockets, every shadow seemed to take on a sinister mening. He thought he saw at least half a dozen different men crouching in odd corners.

There was a stretch between hedges with the football field on one side and some farming land on the other. He had reached there and was beginning to breath more easily when he saw a dark figure break away from the gateway and lurch towards him.

"Now for it!" thought Tom, and he could not help wincing in expectation of the bullet.

The man shambled past.

"Good night!" he grunted, and Tom saw that it was of the cattlemen on his way back to his cottage.

He felt so relieved that he could have laughed out loud. But that made him take a tighter grip on himself, and he walked the rest of the way to the station whistling.

For once the London train was on time, and he soon spotted Gibbs Minor, who was arguing with a porter about his box, which wasin the van.

"I'll see it comes out alright," promised Tom, "You see to your smaller stuff, kid, and collar a taxi. There are only two here this evening."

He made for the baggage car, and almost collided with a shortish, quick-stepping man, who was muffled in a topcoat and just stepped from one of the compartments.

The man grunted something, and hurried on without even looking at the boy, but Tom's blood ran cold, for he had reckonised Nick Stiebel himself, the worst of all the gang, and the man who was now probably their leader.

Nick Stiebel went out through the barrier and entered a waiting car which had drawn up. Tom saw to the box as though in a daze, but he hardly knew what he was doing. He could feel the net closing round him. The whole gang was collecting in the nieghbourhood to carry out vengence on him, and now that Nick had arrived he guessed things would happen.

Somehow Tom himself in a taxi with Gibbs Minor, who was talking away nineteen to the dozen. The younstermust have found his Captain very grumpy and silent during that drive, and ought to have noticed that something was wrong by the way Tom kept looking out from the windows. But Gibbs noticed nothing, not even how Tom shrank back when a big dark-coloured car shot past them about halfway to the school.

Tom knew that car only too well. It belonged to the Grizzlies. They were making for the school, and did not notice him in the taxi.

It was now dark, he did some quick thinking. When they drew up at the school gates and the baggage was being unloaded he would have to pay the driver. He would be exposed in the full view of the headlights, and he guessed what that would mean. If the Grizzlies were nearby he would be riddled.

But what could he do to prevent that? There seemed no way out. He could not—.

Screech! Whizz! Clang!

The Grizzlies' big car had come back round the corner travelling at great speed. The taxi had been in the centre of the road and the driver hardly had time to clap on his brakes and skid to one side. The radiator struck the hedge and the wheel of the passing car tore off one of the mudguards. The car rocked and almost turned over.

Then they were still once more, and the driver was pouring out his woes in colourful language, whilst Gbbs Minor was sitting there as white as a sheet. The big car kept straight on. The Grizzlies did not stop for details like that when they were in a hurry.

"Phew, that was a near one!" Tom heard himself say, "Anybody hurt?"

Nobody was hurt but the taxi man was wrathful at the damage done. He raved and swore he would not move his car from that spot until he had brought the police to see the exact position into which he had been hurled by the passing road-hogs.

Tom backed up this idea. He even offered to go back for the nearest constable, and when ten minutes later he returned with one of the local men he found two or three people standing around talking to the driver.

Without intending to do so, or even know that they had done it, the Grizzlies had solved Tom's problem of how to get back to the school. For the policeman and bystanders all offered to help with Gibbs Minor's baggage, and there was quite a procession of them at the school gate.

Tom hustled Gibbs in as soon as possible, and was not very far behind. He fancied he saw two figures over on the other side of the road in the shadows of some trees, but he was not certain of it. In any case it was too risky even for the Grizzlies to try and attack him with so many people about.

But he was mopping his face when at last he reported to the Head that he had returned safely with Gibbs Minor.

Dr Lumley looked at him rather keenly.

"You've looked rather off-colour lately, Shale! Are you unwell?"

"No, sir!"

"Then are you are worried about something? It's not like you to be so jumpy. You seem to have been worried ever since you returned from visiting yor uncle in Scotland. I hope you have no bad news of him?"

"No, sir, none at all," said Tom, quite truthfully, for he had no uncle in Scotland at all, the gang had invented one in order to get him over to Paris the week before.

Outside the Head's study he straightened his tie and braced his shoulders.

"I shall have to pull my socks up! If everyone can see in my face that I'm jumpy and worried I must look in a mess! Come on, Tom Shale, brace up!"

When he went to see his friends he was as jaunty as could be, and was able to make light of his recent near shave in the taxi.

PART THREE.

THE LAST CHANCE.

It was night time again, and in all the dormitories and sleeping rooms at St Ardens closed eyes and steady breathing made it clear that the pupils were fast asleep. Midnight had struck, and even the whispered conversations so loved by some of the boys after dark had ceased.

Th one exception was in Tom Shale's room, where he lay in bed staring at the window, a revolver in his hand.

He was listening and waiting. He knew perfectly well that Nick Stiebel would not waste a night. If Nick had come down to St Ardens it was because he meant to hurry things up and get rid of this troublesome youngster who had already given them so much bother.

Tom was expecting something to happen, and this time he meant to be ready. He knew that locks and bars could not keep out the Grizzlies, but he had wedged a book under the door of his room, and the gun in his hand was going to be used if necessary. They had forced him to accept it, he would use it against them if they drove him to it.

One o'clock struck, and his eyes had several times closed and opened. He was desperately sleepy, and even his anxiety would not have kept him awake much longer.

Then out in the quad came a deep-throated bark, a snarl, and the sound of a scuffle. Tom sat bolt upright.

It was Rover, the gate-keeper's bulldog, and anyone hearing the little disturbance would take it for granted that Rover had seen a cat and was "seeing it off "the premises.

Tom Sale knew better. He knew it was one or more of the gangsters whom the dog had tackled, and he waited for the expected uproar.

None came. He crept to the window and peered out, careful not to show himself in outline. But it was too dark for him to see anything and he went back and sat on his bed again.

"What happened down there? Has Rover scared them off? It would take more than a dog to scare Stiebel away, I'm thinking."

Another half hour of silence almost convinced him, and then out of the intense silence there suddenly came a rapping at his door, a discreet but unmistakeable knocking.

Tom Shale nearly jumped out of his skin. He pointed the revolver at the door.

"Who—who's there?" he asked.

"It's me—Dick!" came the whispered reply, "Let me in a minute, old chap."

Dick Seymour! He nearly fell with relief.

Thrusting the gun under the pillow, he removed the book from the door and let his pal in. Dick grabbed his arm.

"Don't put the light on. There's something funny going on outside in the quad."

"Something funny?" Tom was startled by the hoarseness of his own voice, "What do you mean?"

"There are men out there. I believe their burglars. About half an hour ago I got up to get a drink of water. As I was getting back into bed I heard Rover let loose at something, and looked from the window. I'm almost certain I saw two men jumping back on top of the wall. I've been watching ever since, and now there are six of themdown at the side door working on it for all they're worth. They're trying to get in."

Trying to get in? Tom's heart nearly stopped.

"Are you sure, Dick?"

"Positive. They're picking the lock or something of that kind. What shall we do? Shall we waken one of the masters? I don't want to scare the kids."

Tom breathed hard.

"No need to waken anyone, old chap. There's a window just over the door in the box-room. Remember it? I noticed when I came past that the housekeeper had left a large bottle of ammonia on the shelf outside the kitchen. Let's give them a dose of that."

He was outwardly cool, inwardly trembling. It was not fear for himself that was shaking him up so much now. He was thinking of the risk his friend and the other boys were running with these human wolvesprowling around with their vengeful errand.

Swiftly the two seniors hastened down the passage to the side door. The gentle scraping continued, and they could hear whispers. At least three or four men were outside, trying to make an entrance. A new lock had been put on since the other night, and they were having some bother with it. But Tom knew nothing of that kind could keep the Grizzlies out very long. He tapped his pal on the arm, and they hurriedly secured the ammonia bottle.

The box-room was not an easy place to move about in when it was dark, but they reached the window at last. It was fastened, and they used every possible care to prevent it squeaking as they slid it open. To give those below the alarm would ruin everything.

At last it was wide enough for the purpose, and Tom Shale cautiously stuck out his head.

There were six of the Grizzlies down there, and Nick Stiebel was the one kneeling at the lock.

Dick passed out the bottle, which was uncorked, and Tom deliberately emptied the contents with a scattering movement over Stiebel and the rest of them.

Then he hastily withdrew.

The ammonia was strong. It burnt the eyes, caught the breath, and nearly choked the Grizzlies. Yelps of amazement and sharp oaths came from the unprepared men. Then came a chorus of sneezes, moans, snuffles, and the scampering of feet.

The boys stuck out their heads, but the stench of ammonia had risen and nearly took away their breadth as well. It was terrifically strong stuff, and must have given the gangsters a terrible time.

Blinded, almost suffocated, they helped each other back over the wall, but a light appeared down at the lodge gates, telling that the keeper had heard something. He was going to come out and see what was happening.

Tom and Dick waited. Dick felt it was a great joke, but Tom was pleased because he knew he had earned another night's reprieve from the sentence the Grizzlies had inflicted on him.

The could now hear the lodge-keeper calling and whistling to his bulldog, but there seemed to be no response. Remembering the silence which had followed the scuffle Tom began to fear seriously for Rover, and his fears were justified.

There was no more disturbances that night, and they went back to their beds to sleep, but in the morning the whole school knew that the lodge-keeper's dog had been killed during the night in the quad. Someone had bashed it's head in with the butt end of a revolver, but not before it had got a bite at someone.

The Grizzlies had not done so well during their midnight visit. That morning burnt eyes and at least one bad bite would testify to their failure.

The news about Rover greatly excited everybody. Once again the police visited the school, and were of the opinion that an attempt had been made to rob the school, but it had been checked by the interruption of the dog.

The ammonia fumes had all drifted away by morning, and the bottle was back on it's shelf, and there was not even a smell to give a hint of what had happened overnight.

Tom was in high spirits that morning. Old Dick had helped him no end the night before, and did not even know it. How he wished he could have told his pal the real truth.

The day passed uneventfully. It was after tea, and the second post was in, when Tom Shale got the worst shock of his life.

Another letter from the gang had come for him, and for a few minutes after reading it the words danced before his eyes.

"We are fed up with the time we're wasting on you. Tonight you'll come to the old rendezvous in the empty house and face the music. Otherwise if you have not turned up by two o'clock in the morning, a bomb will be exploded at your school, and half a dozen of your friends will probaly get theirs as well as you. Make up your mind whether you want to die alone or to bring them into it—Nick Stiebel."

This was indeed the beginning of the end. Tom Shale did not have to make up his mind.

He knew that the gang meant what they said. If he did not appear at the empty house they would not think twice of bombing S Ardens. Was there any way out of this terrible difficulty?

CHAPTER FOURTEEN.

PART ONE.

THE NIGHT GUARD.

It was the end. It was the finish of every thing. Tom Shale could see that.

For months he had bravely kept his secret, and had managed to keep his end up. He had faced all kinds of risks, and had even defied the gang when they had tried to kill him, but now that they had brought others in to it and spoken of killing his school chums he knew it was the finish.

Tom crumpled the letter in his hands and stared at the blank wall. He would have to go to the Headmaster and get him to phone the police. Everything would have to come out, and the police would have to undertake the protection of St Ardens school. They must raid the gang and try to arrest them.

It would mean revealing his own part in the recent affairs, and would uncover the story of his father's life. Those were the very things he had tried to avoid.

But what other way out for the Captain of St Ardens? Until his father's death in Paris he had not even suspected anything. He had always believed his fathr had some business on the continent.

It was the biggest shock of his life when strangers had come to him and proved that his father was "Scarface" Shale, the leader of a notorious gang of crooks known as the Grizzlies. Bigger still was the shock when they had ordered him to take over the leadership of the same gang, threatening him with death and the exposure of his father if he did not agree.

He had agreed in the end, but had privately sworn that he would lead them only for his own ends, and see that they never made a profit out of their schemes.

For months he had carried on the double life, the Captain of St Ardens by day, and more often than not the leader of a gang of crooks at night.

Then they had discovered how he had been tricking them, and how he had secretly been against them all the time, and they had come to St Ardens to put him "on the spot." They had failed in that, and had now sent him this letter. Unless he came to the secret rendezvous that night to take his punishment they were going to explode a bomb at the school and perhaps cause the deaths of many innocent boys.

Tom Shale's chest heaved.

There was nothing else he could do, unless—his face paled at the thought. He could avoid disgrace for himself and his father. He could go to the meeting place they mentioned and let them kill him. Nobody need know why he had been killed, and then neither he nor the school, nor his dead father's name need be smirched.

There was another way out, and of the two he had decided he had better do that.

They had given him until two o'clock in the morning to be at the meeting place. It was already after tea, and it would probably be his last evening on earth.

It was a strange thought. Tom Shale had never tried to imagine what a condemmed man feels like during his last few hours, but now he knew.

He looked out of the window into the quad and saw some boys crossing to the gym, full of life and as happy as could be. Dr Lumley, the Headmaster, had just passed by and had stopped to have a few words with them.

It seemed strange to think he was leaving all this. They had even put him down as captainn of the first eleven in the match against Morden Priory next Saturday, and he had just bought a new pair of football boots.

He looked round the cosy little den which was his by right of the Captaincy of St Ardens, and at the photos and familiar things on the walls. He bit his lip hard. It was going to be very difficult to go away from everything he loved.

But Tom Shale was sufficiently like his father to be able to square his shoulders and face whatever was coming to him. He drew a deep breadth, and just then a knock came on the door. It was one of the juniors to tell him that the Head wanted him in the Master's Common Room.

Tom raised his eyebrows. What was this? Had something come out at last? Was another kind of bomb going to be exploded under his feet? It could not be that he had been found out, or he would have been summoned to Dr Lumley's own room.

He straightened his tie, burnt the letter he had received, and went to the Common Room.

He found most of the masters there as well as the Head. They gave him a seat.

Dr Lumley looked stern.

"We are discussing the things that have recently beenhappening at the school, Shale. I mean the kidnapping of Mr Price, and then the affair of Barber, and the various other alarming incidents, we have had this term. It has been the most disastrous term I have ever known. We have called you in with us because you are the senior boy, and we want your help."

"Yes, sir."

"It seems to us that all this could not have happened unless there was an influence at work in the school. It is possible that some unfortunate boy is mixed up with a gang of evil men, or in some way has become connected with them."

Tom's heart thumped madly. The Head was getting hot on the scent.

"Last night there was an attempted burglarly, and the gate-keeper's dog was brutally killed. The school seems to be the centre of the ativities of a gang of lawbreakers and naturally we have to put a stop to it, Shale. Have you any reason to believe that any of the boys is in trouble outside the school?"

"No, sir, said Tom, honestly,"I don't believe any of them are. They're a fine lot of chaps. And—."

There were murmers of approval from the Masters. They had seemingly already decided the same thing. Dr Lumley spread his arms.

"Then I am at a lose to understand many things. I have been to the police so many times this term that I am ashamed to go to them again. Yet I feel the school has not finished with those weird happenings. I am going to raise a volunteer guard to watch the school at nights. The Masters have all offered their services, and I want just two or three of you older boys to make up the dozen. Can you suggest two others?"

"Yes, sir, I know Dick Seymour and Reddy Trotter would gladly enlist, and they wouldn't talk to the others about the affair, sir."

"Good! I don't want the whole school alarmed. Tonight we won't worry them, but maybe you will join three of the Masters in forming a corden in the grounds. You can all be armed with Indian clubs from the gymnasium, and keep a two hour watch in pairs. That will divide the night equally."

Tom nodded, then was forced to listen to the setting of the final details. Eventually, he found that he was to be with Mr Gorden, the science master, from midnight until two o'clock, and he was to say nothing to anybody else about it.

Not until he was outside in the corridor did he remember that he had to be at the meeting place of the gang by two o'clock at the latest, otherwise the bomb would exploded before dawn.

"This puts a stopper on it! He muttered, "I could have slipped away from the school at any ordinary time, but how in the name of wisdom can I do it if Gorden is tacked on to me?"

It began to look more and more certain to him that he would have to make a clean breast of affairs, but hoping against hope, he hung on and did not do anything rash.

PART TWO.

THE TRIAL.

Before lights out that evening Tom had decided what to do. He would make a clean breast of things, but there was a better way than going to the Head. He could imagine Dr Lumley's horror, and the reproaches he would heap upon his head. Tom Shale knew he could not stand that, so he made up his mind to go straight to the police.

To them he could answer to some extent for what he had done by leading them to the empty house not so very far away where the gang had their headquarters. If he helped to capture the gang he would feel that he had done something to keep his own end up, even if he was expelled and went to prison for what he had done.

He was advised to get a couple of hours sleep before his turn of duty in the grounds commenced, but Tom did not go to bed. He knew the side door was not locked until after ten, and he merely went up one staircase and down the another.

A few minutes later he was in the quad, and sneaking across to the favourite tree which gave him a chance to get over the wall into the road.

The lights in the dormitories had gone out. The school was in darkness except in the Master's Common Room. He droped lightly on his toes from the top of the wall, and drew a deep breath.

A quarter of an hour would see him at the village police station. They would have to phone for reinforcements before they tackled the Grizzlies' hideout, and it would probably be half-past eleven or midnight before they reached the house.

Now that he had made up his mind he felt happier. He started off briskly, but had not gone fifty yards from the gateway before two dark figures closed in on him so suddenly he did not even have time to clench his fists.

"So you've come! Always knew you had gutsif nothing else, you little double-crosser!"

Something hard was pressed against his side. He did not need to look down because h knew what it was. It was a revolver held in the hand of Nick Stiebel, one of the leaders of the gang, and the other man also belonged to the Grizzlies.

"I—i—! he began.

"Save your breath!" hissed Stiebel, "There's a car waiting, and everyone is at the house. We'll give you a trial. March!"

The revolver prodded him on, and he had to obey. He was rather in a daze. It had all happened so quickly. The gangsters had been waiting outside the school to escort him to his place of execution, and they had known the tree he usually used to cross the wall.

The car was round the bend, with a third man at the wheel, and he was pushed inside, he remembered the day some months ago when he had been taken in similar fashion to face the gang and be told of his father's death.

That had been rather different. The gang had looked upon him as a mere boy then, and had preferred him as a leader to splitting up their numbers by having a quarrel over who should lead them.

Now they knew he had been working against them all the time, and they would be merciless.

Nick Stiebel had never liked him, and now he showed his dislike by never taking the gun away for an instant as they sped down the lanes.

"We always told you the punishment for a traitor in our bunch!" he said grimly, "Scarface himself would have agreed with you being shot for this."

Tom wondered. He doubted whether his father had even considered the possibility of his own folly falling upon the head of his son. But it was no good arguing. Tom tightened his lips and said nothing during the rest of the journey.

The house was the same, and when he was ushered into the big room in the basement a growl came from the dozen or so men assembled there. The gang was in full force, he could not see anyone was missing.

"Dirty traitor! Skunk! Little rat!"

Those and many other names were hurled at him.

"Put him on the spot, Nick."

Slim Dolman pushed his lean length to the front.

"Wait a minute. Give the kid a chance to speak. Everyone has achance to do that in this gang."

Nick and Slim glared at each other. There was not much love lost between these two. But on this occasion Nick agreed, and Tom was pushed to the centre of the room.

The tight-lipped crooks all fixed their eyes on him, and some of them fidgetted with the guns in their pockets. Nick sat down beside a small black bag and patted it with one hand.

"Lucky for your school you came! There's a powerful enough bomb here to blow up one whole wing of St Ardens. You wouldn't have died alone. Now is there anything you want to say before we put you against the wall."

Tom felt surprisingly cool. This shadow had been over him for so long that he was almost pleased that the end had come.

He faced them boldly.

"Only this, that it wasn't fair to pick on a chap at school who had never heard of you and try and make him work in with you. Everyone of you joined the gang of his own accord and ought to have been loyal to it, but I was forced into it, and couldn't be expected to feel the same as you do. I'm not a crook."

"Your the son of one," growled someone, and Tom flushed.

"Maybe, but he didn't bring me up to be one. He was a good father to me, and he must have had his reasons for going wrong. Anyway, what's the point of arguing? You don't intend to give me a chance. You intend to shoot me, so go ahead."

he felt much the same as when he had been outside the Head's door waiting for a licking.

The gang began to get up, and many of them drew guns. There was a bare wall at theend of the room. In a few minutes he would be standing there as a target for their shots.

Nick Stiebel and Slim Dolman were arguing. Slim seemed to be siding with Tom over something.

"......it was quite he was forced into it!" he said, "Why not shanghai him abroad somewhere as we did with that kid called Barber? By the time he returns we'll have made a clean-up and seperated. Anyway, he won't split on us for fear of giving himself away."

A growl of disagreement came from the others

"No, Nick is right. Let's give him what he deserves here and now. Get it over. The dirty little pup has cost us thousands of pounds during the last few months, and we never guessed why we were "unlucky". Shoot him."

The argument rose louder, and two of the gang pulled Tom to the bare wall. Both Nick and Slim had their guns out facing each other. Already they were beginning their old quarrel as to who should have the loudest say in the conduct of the gang.

Tom at first had listened dully, but now as the clamour increased he began to get a new idea. He had been led into that basement room through a large and solid-looking door. Om the outside he had seen a key.

If he made a quick dash for it he might even get outside, slam it on them, and lock them in long enough to drive their car to the police station. His father had taught hi to drive long ago.

Tom drew a deep breath. His fighting spirit was up. There was only one man in the way and as he looked in the opposite direction for an instant the youngster slammed him on the side of the jaw and lept past him to the door.

He was outside and banged the door closed before the first hot rang out. Then came a perfect fusilade from the angry gangsters, but the door was solid enough to stop the bullets, and he turned the big key without any trouble.

Bang! Crash!

The noise on the other side was tremendous. He lost no time listening, sprinted up the stairs, and bolted the other door on the outside. That would check them for a little longer.

Then out through the front door of the house to the car in the driveway. He felt like whooping as he clambered into the driving seat. At least he would not die like a rat in a trap, and he would get the police on the scene soon enough to round up some of the bunch.

He pressed the starter again and again, before he realised he had not switched on. He remedied this, and tried once more. The warm engine purred over, and he was about to let in the clutch when.....

Boom!

The most terrific explosion he had ever heard occurred in the basement of the house behind him.

He turned his head in wonder, in time to see part of the wall split apart and a vivid fork of flame shoot skywards. Then mortar and bricks began to crash down on the car.

He ducked his head and waited, but although the windows were smashed and plenty of stuff fell onto the road he wasn't hurt.

White-faced, he clambered out and stared at the ruined house. Not a sound came from it's depths the whole gang must have been instantly killed in that confined space. It was ompossible that anyone could have lived under there.

"Gosh! What happened?

The question was unanswerable. Nobody would ever know what had happened down there.

Either the gangsters during their quarrel had knocked the bomb from the table and exploded it that way, or it had exploded accidently through some fault in the making.

The fact remained it had blown them and the house to pieces, and Tom stood there quite three minutes before the fact dawned on him he was finally free.

Free!

He would not heve to go to the police. He would not have to go to the Head. If he could get back to the school before midnight and take his spell with the science master he might successfully leave his past life behind him.

He started to run, choosing the short cut across the fields, and it was on his way back to the school that he remembered the one thing that could give him away.

At one time the gang had brought off a raid unknown to Tom, and without his consent had sent him a large sum of money as his share of the profits. Not knowing what to do with it he hid it in a book in his study, and one of the boys named Jeff Barber, from the Fifth, had seen him put it there.

Jeff Barber had been a bit of an outsider, and in the debt to a bookmaker down in the village. He had fallen to the temptation of stealing some of the money and giving it to the bookie.

Unfortunately for him the notes were stolen ones the numbers of which were known, and he was arrested.

He had refused to say where he had got the money, but the Grizzlies had been afraid he might give away their leader and hd kidnapped him and shanghaied him on a steamer sailing for South America. He should be back soon, and if he liked to tell about the notes in Tom's book he could make things unpleasant for the Captain of St Ardens.

PART THREE.

A MYSTERY FOR THE POLICE.

But for the time being there was no danger of that, and Tom regained the school grounds without being discovered. Then came the problem of getting back to the his room before ten minutes to twelve, when he was to be called to take his turn on sentry duty.

He was saved even that trouble. There was a light in the gymnasium, and when he peeped in through the window he saw Mr Gordon selecting a couple of Indian clubs.

Tom could not help grinning. Mr Gordon was taking his duties quite seriously, but to heve left the building at such a time he must have unlocked a door. It would still be open for him to return.

This was the case, and Tom crept back to his own room, and after getting rid of his dirty boots lay down on the bed with a rug over him to await his call.

He was trembling a little now that it was all over, and when he remembered all he had gone through that night he felt his heart beating more than ever. To have narrowly escaped a violent death, and then to have seen a dozen men blown up by a bomb was not excatly the quietest way of spending a night.

It seemed only a few minutes later when Mr Gordon came and softly called him.

"Time, Shale! We've got to take over our duties now."

"I'll be ready in two ticks, sir," whispered back Tom, and a few minutes later he was creeping down the stairs armed with an Indian club.

At any other time he might have felt excited with the prospect of this night watch, but now he knew perfectly well that nothing was going to happen.

There would be no more mysterious happenings at St Ardens, no more midnight visitors, no more attempts to enter the school and kidnap either master or boys. That would be a thing of the past.

The two hours seemed endless. He was yawning long before it was over, and then two of the other masters solemnly took over from them and learned that it all was quiet.

The fresh air and the company of Mr Gordon had done Tom good. This time when he went to bed he no longer shook, and his ears had forgotten the roar of the exploding bomb. He was soon asleep, and did not waken till calling bell.

All the school was excited that morning by the news which had come of a mysterious explosion in an empty house a couple of miles away during the night. Someone had heard the noise even at St Ardens but had thought it was motor-car tyre exploding.

The police and the fire brigade had been on the scene within twenty minutes, and had been labouring among the ruins all night. It was rumoured that they had found bodies, but the place was so utterly destroyed that they could not make much headway.

Tom breathed more easily. He was not a bit sorry for the Grizzlies, except maybe Slim Dolman, who unsuspectingly saved Tom's life by starting that quarrel. But even Slim was a crook like the rest of them who would not hesitate even at murder if it served his ends.

So the day went on, and the events of the night seemed to get dimmer and dimmer in Tom's memory. He did his best to forget everything, and to interest himself only in his classes and his school pals, but he did not get real ease of mind until about a month later he heard two masters talking about a letter the Head had received from Jeff Barber's parents.

Evidently the shanghaid youngster had managed to escape from the ship and communicate with his parents. His father had written to say rather than allow his son to return and face the shame of further investigations he had arranged for him to go to a distant cousin who had a farm in Mexico.

So far as Tom was concerned his connection with the underworld of crime was over, and he had made up his mind that he would never make his father's mistake of getting mixed up with anything crooked as long as he lived.

Memory of those nights when he had expected a summons from the Grizzlies, and of the time when he had feared discovery every hour, made Tom Shale determined to lead the most honest of lives.

There was a certain amount of money left in trust for him by his father, but he decided that as part of it was undoubtedly stolen he would use as little as possible.

Thaat was why he shortly afterwards chose to go into th Navy, rather than go on further with his education. He wanted to be able to earn his own living as soon as possible and send the money to charities.

The mystery of the dozen bodies found in the ruins of the empty house was never solved, although the police gave it out that some revolutionaries must have been working on a bomb and had been blown up by their own invention.

Certainly nobody at St Ardens right up to the day when they bade farewell to their popular Captain, ever suspected that Tom Shale had been the sole witness of the affair or how near he had been to being " on the spot " that fateful night.

And there was no more exciting and mysterious happenings at the school, much to the relief of Dr Lumley.

THE END.